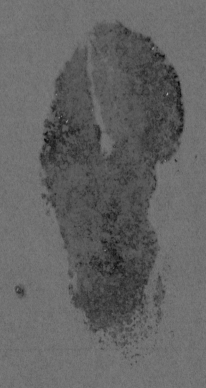

A
HARD
MAN
TO
KILL

**MIDNIGHT
NOVEL OF
SUSPENSE**

Also by Ritchie Perry

THE FALL GUY

A
HARD
MAN
TO
KILL

Ritchie Perry

Houghton Mifflin Company Boston
1973

FIRST PRINTING C

Printed in the United States of America

Library of Congress Cataloging in Publication Data

Perry, Ritchie, 1942–
    A hard man to kill.

    (A Midnight novel of suspense)
    I. Title.
PZ4.P4646Har3 [PR6066.E72]   823'.9'14   73-6700
ISBN 0-395-17204-7

A
HARD
MAN
TO
KILL

Plevny, Poland, June 1943

The body of Private Herbert Brunnig was found in a small copse outside the village of Plevny, with nearly thirty stab wounds in his back. All these wounds had been inflicted by a frenzied twelve-year-old boy, demented because at the time of his death Brunnig had been raping the child's mother. Colonel Klemper did not know who had killed Brunnig or why. This did not concern him. What did was that a soldier under his command had been murdered in the vicinity of the village, an act which demanded immediate retribution. One hundred and sixty-three people, men, women and children, were burned to death in the wooden village church, incinerated on the orders of Colonel Klemper because Herbert Brunnig, Private, drunkard and rapist, had been killed. This execution was deemed necessary for the honor and maintenance of the Third Reich.

Only one person in the entire village escaped the holocaust, the same twelve-year-old who had stabbed the soldier more than two dozen times. The boy had fled into the woods directly afterward, the bloodstained knife still clutched in his hand. When hunger eventually forced him back to his home, the inhabitants of Plevny and their village church were no more than a heap of smoking ashes. This boy's name was Jan Miteck.

Madrid, Spain, December 1971

Roger Brookes was drinking his second cup of coffee, an integral part of the regular morning metamorphosis, completing his transformation from a grunting, monosyllabic subhuman into a reasonable facsimile of an alert executive. His wife had a simple explanation for the phenomenon, seeing it as the point where her husband came to terms with his daily hangover, but it was an opinion she kept to herself. When the telephone rang in the livingroom, Brookes was returning the empty cup to its saucer.

'I'll get it,' he said, pushing himself up from the kitchen chair.

The conversation was brief, lasting little more than a minute. Then Brookes returned to the kitchen to collect the jacket draped over the back of his chair.

'It's the office,' he explained. 'Apparently there's a flap on.'

His wife nodded resignedly and poured herself another cup of coffee.

'Try not to be late tonight,' she asked. 'We've promised to go to the Hendersons for dinner.'

'Don't worry,' Brookes assured her, bending to plant a quick peck on his wife's forehead. 'I'll make a point of being home early.'

Despite his promise, Brookes didn't have dinner with the Hendersons that night, although the omission was hardly his fault. What he'd failed to appreciate, couldn't possibly have known, was that his secretary had made the call summoning him to the office with a knife held menacingly at her throat. Nor could Brookes have known that while his secretary had been on the phone Heinrich Klemper had been carefully examining the contents of the filing cabinet. In fact, once he'd left the flat, Mrs. Brookes never saw her husband again.

Tel Aviv, Israel, December 1971

'Why?' General Brinkmann asked curiously. 'Not that I've any intention of accepting your resignation, but I am interested in the reasons for your request.'

'Klemper has surfaced at last,' Miteck answered curtly.

Brinkmann nodded his head thoughtfully, requiring no further explanation. Nevertheless, he was uncertain of the best line to adopt and scrutinized the other man appraisingly, knowing the naturalized Pole was far too valuable a man to lose. For a non-Jew to have risen so high was testimony enough to his ability, and officers of his experience were essential assets in the confused situation, the near turmoil that had arisen since Nasser's death.

'How long is it now, Jan?'

Brinkmann was still uncertain of his approach.

'Twenty-eight years, as if you didn't know.'

Although he was barely forty, Miteck was already beginning to look like an old man, great purple smudges under his eyes, his thin, heavily lined face a muddy gray. In contrast, Brinkmann, fifteen years the senior, seemed positively youthful.

'You've been very patient,' the General commented.

'I've had to be,' was the terse reply.

When Brinkmann laughed it was without amusement.

'It's ironic,' he said. 'Six months ago, in the same circumstances, there would have been no question of resignation. I would have been able to offer you every assistance.

Now my hands are tied. It's hardly the time to risk annoying the Americans.'

'That's your problem, General,' Miteck answered, unimpressed. 'I intend to kill Klemper.'

'You'll throw away your whole career?'

Before Miteck nodded, Brinkmann knew what the answer would be, secretly in full sympathy with his subordinate. Even so, he had to be dissuaded, his craving for vengeance deferred to affairs of greater importance. As always, Brinkmann had the appropriate compromise at his fingertips.

England, January 1972

The creak of the door seemed deafening, and for tense seconds Tracey remained rooted to the spot, afraid to move, sweat trickling down his face despite the cold. Klemper had stirred uneasily at the sudden noise, rolling over in bed, but gradually the even tenor of his breathing resumed and Tracey thought it prudent to slip out onto the landing, closing the door carefully behind him. For the first time he was able to use his pocket light, following the narrow beam down the stairs, then across the hall to the study. Twenty minutes later Tracey was so absorbed with the combination lock to the safe he was unaware that Klemper had come into the room. If he had known, Tracey would have regretted the fact that his equipment did not include a suicide capsule.

1

IT WAS A BITTERLY COLD DAY, the kind when brass monkeys collapsed screaming in the gutter and had to be given the kiss of life. One of those crisp and frosty mornings which used to send Victorian poets scurrying for their quill pens and made me wish I'd stayed in bed. It certainly wasn't the weather for driving, not on icily treacherous country roads in a vehicle I'd never handled before. The tires of the milk van had looked suspiciously bald when I'd examined them at the depot and on every corner they were happy to prove this wasn't one of the cases where appearances were deceptive. From choice I wouldn't have taken the van over twenty, mindful that there was enough glass behind to cut me to ribbons if I crashed, but orders were orders and I actually managed to reach the manor a couple of minutes ahead of schedule. With a last four-wheel skid the van screeched to a halt, the hood almost touching the trellised metal gates, and I gave a peremptory blast on the horn.

There was a minute's delay, then the gateman sauntered out of the lodge looking considerably more convincing in his role than I felt in my peaked cap and white jacket. It was probably the shotgun that did the trick because Ralph Bates had been living with firearms since his days in Korea. To add to his army experience he had muscle and he had brains, which was why he was playing at gateman for a so-called eccentric millionaire in Kent. His employer was eccentric all right, although I could think of better adjectives to describe him.

To his eternal discredit, Bates disliked me on sight, instantly wary because I was a break with routine. Ostentatiously he adjusted his hold on the scatter gun. Although it wasn't actually pointing at me, it was close enough for him to make his point.

'You're new,' he said.

It was an accusation, not a question.

'That's right,' I confessed. 'The regular man is down with flu.'

Bates inspected me coldly, neither believing nor disbelieving what I'd said. In his own way he was a good man, which made it all the more regrettable that he'd chosen the wrong side. Moving unhurriedly, he trudged back to the lodge and I lit a cigarette. From the length of time he was gone, he must have checked with the depot, fortunately one of the contingencies we'd allowed for in the timetable. When he did return, Bates's attitude showed he was well aware the phone call proved nothing, merely removed a possibility, and he didn't allow me to proceed even after the gates were closed behind me.

'I'll take a look inside,' he informed me. 'It's the boss's orders.'

He could see most of the van's interior from where he was standing and didn't think for a moment that I had a passenger aboard. Nevertheless, I climbed down from the cab while Bates watched closely for any telltale bulges in my clothing. Although there weren't any, there was still my moneybag and he didn't intend to overlook a thing. If

I did have a gun concealed in the bag, I was hardly likely to haul it out while he was facing me with the shotgun, so he turned his back to climb into the van, swinging round almost immediately, his gun cocked and pointing at my stomach. Anticipating this, I hadn't moved and Bates relaxed visibly.

'You can carry on now,' he said, offering no word of apology, although he did condescend to lower the muzzle of the shotgun.

There didn't seem to be much point in answering. Bates still thought my hand was going up to remove the cigarette from my mouth when a bullet from the derringer entered his right eye, the tiny gun making almost no noise in the cold, morning air. It was one of the tricks of the trade Bates had learnt only when it was too late, and he was dead before his face could register the chagrin he would have felt. If he'd considered the possibility of a spring holster strapped to the inside of my right forearm, he would never have turned his back for a second. Now he'd never know his mistake.

Jumping back into the van, I grabbed the screwdriver from the glove compartment and undid the screws securing the false floor. Soames handed up my shoulder holster, gun and silencer, then squeezed himself out. He was cold and cramped from the journey, more than relieved that the dangerous part of his piece of the action was over. While I slipped off my jacket and put on the shoulder rig, Soames dragged Bates into the lodge. As I restarted the engine I could see him through the window, already on the phone to tell the house that the new milkman had passed muster.

It was nearly half a mile from the gate to the house and

the van handled much better on the gravel of the drive. Even so, I didn't hurry myself. Up till this point I was slightly ahead of schedule and the last thing I wanted to do was to leave myself out on a limb by arriving too early.

As befitted my status as a common tradesman, I drove the van round to the rear of the house, a Victorian monstrosity amid its acres of rime-covered park, and, until I reached the porch, I was the perfect milkman, whistling jauntily as I crunched over the gravel, the milk basket clutched in my left hand. Once I was satisfied I couldn't be seen from any of the windows, I began to destroy my image, unholstering my gun and screwing the silencer into place before I rang the bell. The man who opened the door wouldn't have been everyone's idea of the perfect butler and he certainly wasn't mine. He looked more like a second-rate wrestler, which was exactly what his file said he'd once been.

'How many pints today, sir?' I asked politely, jamming the gun into his stomach.

He'd been around long enough not to argue and, after a quick grunt of surprise, he backed into the kitchen without any fuss. The middle-aged woman standing by the sink, the room's only other occupant, was no dewy-eyed innocent either. When she saw the gun in my hand she didn't think of screaming, fainting, or anything feminine like that. Instead her hand began sliding toward a wicked-looking meat knife on the draining board beside her.

'Forget it, love,' I said quietly. 'Shooting you won't bother me at all.'

She didn't realize how sensible she was when she did as I'd instructed. It was an extermination mission, with only one person in the house whose life was important. Apart from mine, that is. Delving into my moneybag, I brought out a package of adhesive tape and tossed it across to the woman.

'Stick a slab of that across your rosebud mouth, Beryl,' I ordered. 'Then you can immobilize Wally.'

Although she bristled her mustache at me, Beryl obeyed my instructions and, after she'd finished with Wally, I made her tape her own legs together before I went over to deal with her hands. As soon as both of them were safely deposited in a convenient cupboard, I used the time in hand to strip off the milkman gear. The change made me feel almost human again. Scared human admittedly, but definitely human.

Dead on time I heard the sound of Peter approaching in the helicopter, the engine missing badly. He was very low over the house, the rotors making an infernal din, and the building suddenly came alive. Doors banged, footsteps pounded down the stairs and there was a babble of excited voices, all of which might be expected when a helicopter makes a forced landing on the front lawn.

To my relief the noise of the rotors died without the explosion I'd been half expecting, and I uncrossed my fingers. Three people had run through the front door, meaning they hadn't forgotten in the excitement to leave two men upstairs. In stockinged feet I crept silently along the stone-flagged corridor. There was nobody in the entrance hall and I crouched beneath the stairs, listening carefully. At first I could hear nothing, apart from the voices outside, where Peter was doing a grand job keeping the bulk of the opposition enthralled with his intrepid bird-man spiel. Acutely aware of the time element, I was on the point of breaking cover when there was a creak directly above which stopped me in my tracks. It meant one of the men who'd remained in the house was stationed on the landing, and I was effectively stymied. We had banked on one man staying with Tracey, two I could possibly have dealt with, but not with one of them on the landing. Precious seconds ticked by and there was no inspiration. In less than five minutes the balloon was due to go up, Tracey as good as dead unless I could take out the guards. The problem was that if the man on the landing gave the alarm, or even died noisily, the second guard would kill the prisoner.

Quietly I ran back down the corridor, through the kitchen and out into the garden. The pillars of the porch I dismissed at the first glance and pressed onward, running hard round the side of the house, the frozen gravel biting cruelly into my unprotected feet. Peter had the other three men by the grounded helicopter, still explaining what had gone wrong, and I hoped he could hold their attention. It only needed one of them to turn his head and we were finished.

The wisteria that grew over the front façade was probably as old as the house itself and I climbed it fast, my gun jammed uncomfortably down the front of my trousers. To my surprise I reached a first-floor window without any shouts from the lawn. Hanging precariously on to the wisteria with one hand, I brought out my pocketknife with the other, prayed Soames had remembered to switch off the alarm system from the lodge and slipped the catch. The sash itself was stiff, requiring a full thirty seconds before I could push it high enough to clamber inside, thirty seconds I could ill afford.

According to my calculations I should have left one of the guards on the landing below, but I was a long way from being home and dry, for by now Soames would have opened the gate to the rest of Pawson's men. And, to make things easier, it was an old house, a creak in every other board. Moving both quickly and silently was out of the question, which meant I had to contain my impatience and make the best speed I could. There were bare seconds left when I reached the room where Tracey should be and, before I tried it, I knew the door had to be locked. It was that sort of a day. A crafty peek through the keyhole was no go either. All I could see was key.

I knew I wasn't fast enough, come to that I didn't think anyone could be, but I had to try just the same. One bullet sufficed to shoot off the lock, then I hurled myself into the room, head swiveling to locate the guard. We fired simultaneously. My shot hit the guard in the stomach, the impact of the bullet driving him back through the window in a welter of glass and splintered wood. For my part I was unscathed, mainly because nobody had fired at me. Instead the guard had shot the naked man strapped to the bed, the new wound barely noticeable among the mass of tortured flesh.

Feeling sick, not least because I'd failed, I was hardly aware of the spatter of gunfire outside. The sound of footsteps rushing upstairs was a different matter. The second guard was my responsibility and, although I suspected Tracey was already dead, I didn't intend to risk any more shooting near him. Gun in hand, I stood by the open door listening to the approaching footsteps until, at the last corner, they stopped. Unscrewing the silencer from my gun, I counted slowly to thirty before I threw myself out of the door in a rolling dive, firing as I went. The first two bullets were purely for effect, and did no more than make a devil of a lot of noise and ruin the wallpaper. The next two were the ones that mattered, fired after I'd spotted the doorway the man was sheltering in and while he was still wondering why I'd left the room. It was all very well for him to follow the textbook, just his hard luck I'd read it too. He'd been so certain I'd be waiting for him in the room he'd managed only one reflex shot, missing me by a mile.

The dust brushed from my trousers, I went back into the room and across to the bed. Incredibly Tracey was still alive, holding on to a last, faint flicker of life, his pain-racked breathing clearly audible now that the shooting outside had ceased. Gently I cradled his head on my arm, wiping away a trickle of blood from the corner of his mouth.

'Geoffrey,' I whispered. 'It's Philis.'

Slowly his eyes opened, startlingly blue against the wreckage of his face. Recognition dawned as they focused on me.

'What did you learn?' I asked urgently, knowing I didn't have long. 'Pawson has to know.'

With a dreadful effort Tracey's mouth opened, his swollen lips struggling to form the syllables. Then, instead of words, there was a great gout of blood, running over his chin and onto his bare chest. Somehow, with his last breath, he gasped a single word before his head lolled to the side and he was dead.

Back on my feet I turned away from his body and walked to the window, sick to my stomach, so nauseated I couldn't vomit. A small group of men was approaching the house across the frost-whitened grass and I knew I couldn't face them for the moment. Quietly I ran down the stairs and slipped out of the back door, stopping only to retrieve my shoes. One of the men shouted to me as I drove past in the milk van but I ignored him. All I wanted to do was get away. A long way away where I wouldn't have to think about Tracey.

The public bar of the Turk's Head was packed with lunch-time revelers, a leavening of secretaries and receptionists to brighten the dark-suited anonymity of the businessmen. It was no coincidence that whereas the other tables were crowded I sat alone, projecting an aura of antisociability which made people notice the three empty chairs round me and decide they'd rather stand after all. One girl, sporting a miniskirt which drew unwanted attention to her tree-trunk thighs, had been braver than most, but it had taken her less than five minutes to move.

However, my black mood was an ideal opportunity for Pawson, giving him a chance to demonstrate how well he knew his men, for if he'd sent anyone else but Peter I would have told him to run away and play with himself. The choice also provided a perfect illustration of another facet of Pawson's character. Peter had taken a bullet through the shoulder during the morning's fiasco, and only one of nature's born grade-A bastards would have sent him out again the same day.

'Hallo, Philis,' he said somberly, his tone designed to fit in with the way I felt.

I sneered at him to show how much I appreciated his company, and swallowed another mouthful of light and bitter. Although I wouldn't have dreamed of admitting the fact, I was glad Peter had come, public school upbringing and all.

'How do you feel now?' he asked, endeavoring to establish contact.

'I'm all right,' I told him. 'I only wish I could say the same about Tracey.'

My glass was empty and I forced my way to the bar to buy another pint. As a new arrival Peter had to make do with a half.

'You shouldn't blame yourself, Philis,' Peter said once I was back, wiping froth from his top lip.

'I don't. Tracey is reserved for Pawson's conscience, not mine.'

Peter realized I wasn't at my most cooperative and cast around in his mind for a more rewarding approach. His meditation lasted long enough for me to dispose of half of my beer.

'I didn't see Tracey myself,' he remarked at last, 'but they told me he was in a pretty bad state.'

The understatement made me laugh, a harsh, unpleasant laugh that had several heads turning in our direction. Most of them turned away quickly when they saw the expression on my face.

'They told you that, did they? I don't know how you classify pretty bad but I've never seen anything like it. Someone at the manor must have had the ABC book of torture because Klemper's ghouls didn't miss out a thing. Not that I noticed anyway.' I paused, a nasty taste in my mouth as I remembered what had been done to Tracey. 'You know, Peter, until today I couldn't stand Tracey. I thought he was a miserable, pretentious creep. It didn't have anything to do with him being homosexual, it was just that I couldn't understand what he was doing in the department. Now I know. He took everything, blowlamp, pliers, the lot, and he held on until he could tell someone what he'd found out. The poor, brave, little sod.'

It wasn't much of an obituary but it was the best I could manage under the circumstances and Peter appreciated how I felt, even if the words themselves didn't amount to a great deal. Our drinks finished, he handed me the money for another round, the sling on his right arm preventing him from collecting them himself. Several minutes passed before he reopened the conversation.

'What did Tracey say?' he asked. 'Could he tell you much?'

'Just one word, a name, but it's enough,' I told him.

It had to be. Since the morning this was one assignment for which I could muster considerable enthusiasm.

A good night's sleep worked wonders. By the next morning my mood of the previous day was a thing of the past, my anger carefully filed away for future reference, leaving me ready for the business of day-to-day living, a return to the hypocrisy, schmaltz and double-dealing involved in my work for SR(2). The letters in the department's name stood for Special Responsibilities, the intelligence world's equivalent of the silk purse–pig's ear syndrome, and the number was a meaningless appendage, unless it was a proclamation of independence from British Rail. As far as I could see, the only special feature of the department was its complete lack of a specific function, something which branded it as a pariah. Espionage was for DI6, counterespionage was the province of DI5 and, to a lesser extent, of Special Branch. The roles of the various service units were

self-explanatory, as were the functions of the two new in-
dustrial intelligence sections, and even the Inland Revenue
could justify its existence, providing living proof that the
principles behind the Gestapo were not yet dead. SR(2),
on the other hand, lacked any clear sense of purpose.
Theoretically it was nothing more than a glorified police
auxiliary, responsible only to the Home Secretary. In practice it all too often operated to the rear of the larger
agencies, tidying up the mess they left behind. The sole
occasions on which it appeared in the front line, hatchet
jobs like the one the previous day, were when there was a
fair chance of a nasty kickback. In the armed forces,
SR(2) would have been on permanent latrine duty.

Keenly aware of this, I normally made a point of not
arriving at work before ten, but the morning after Tracey's
death I entered the appropriately undistinguished building
off Queen Victoria Street at five minutes to nine. Susan
Sherwood, beautiful, efficient and available, the perfect
secretary for any man except me, was already at her post.
For me she was an exceptionally tantalizing piece of bait,
provided courtesy of Pawson, about as safe to handle as
Typhoid Mary. From the expression on her face as I came
in I could tell the office grapevine had been working overtime, another triumph for internal security.

'Good morning, Mr. Philis,' she greeted me, her boudoir
smile revealing a set of exquisitely capped teeth. 'I didn't
expect to see you so early.'

'Good morning, Miss Sherwood,' I said in my most
formal tone, not breaking stride until I had my office door
closed behind me.

The office, a majestic room some ten feet square, last
decorated at the turn of the century, had belonged to me

for little over a month and, theoretically, I should have been bursting with pride at my rise in the hierarchy. Certainly I had no complaints about the increase in salary and expenses, particularly as there had been no corresponding increase in my workload. My unspoken complaint was that the promotion helped to make a vision of normal life outside the department ever more unreal. Much as I hated to admit it, I was with Pawson to stay.

To brighten the morning there were four files awaiting attention on my desk. Three of them were bulky, technical tracts, totally incomprehensible without an interpreter or a B.Sc. Having neither, I initialed them without bothering to read beyond the title pages. The fourth, a brief précis of the annual amendments to standing orders, made for equally fascinating reading and received similar treatment. With the folders stacked neatly in the OUT tray, the morning's paperwork was finished, and I was halfway through the football reports in the *Mirror* when I was disturbed by a tap at the door.

After I'd shouted for her to come in, Miss Sherwood glided the few steps toward me, breasts jiggling so provocatively it wouldn't have surprised me to learn she went through a couple of brassieres a week. There was no earthly reason why she couldn't have remained on the far side of the desk but, being Miss Sherwood, she chose to stand as close as possible without actually sitting on my lap. Already she'd made it perfectly clear that the only thing standing between us and bed was my failure to ask; now she was becoming desperate, wondering how long it would be before I finally weakened, admitted that sexy, full-breasted honey blondes didn't leave me completely cold. Normally my natural sense of chivalry would have made me more than cooperative, but I'd been puzzled by Pawson's motives in treating me to the most desirable secretary in London, and I had contrived to get my hands on her personnel file. The answer had become instantly apparent. Nobody in his right mind would knowingly lay Pawson's niece, not if he worked for SR(2).

'Mr. Pawson would like to see you, sir,' she said respectfully, giving my elbow an affectionate squeeze with her thighs.

'I'm busy at the moment,' I told her, disengaging my arm. 'You'd better say I'll be up in ten minutes.'

She glanced at my *Daily Mirror,* giggled, licked her lips sexily, and went out, waving her rear suspension at me on the way. Stimulating as the sight undoubtedly was, I knew I had to arrange for her to be transferred. Otherwise I feared for my sanity.

The sports section finished, I leaned back in my chair to devote some thought to Schnellinger's stupidity. He'd been running a nice, cozy little operation, selling information to everyone from the Albanians to the Zambians, the kind of impartial service nobody could seriously object to. He'd been reliable, discreet and not too expensive, in fact a positive asset. Then, seduced by American gold, Schnellinger had gone off the rails. The real responsibility lay with the Americans, their mistaken belief that the cause of world peace could best be served by turning Schnellinger's outfit into an adjunct of the CIA. This had been a very shortsighted view indeed. While Schnellinger had been at everyone's beck and call he'd been left well alone. He'd naturally wanted to stay incognito and nobody had pried too closely, chiefly because he was so well hidden. Every country which had anything to lose was losing a little to Schnellinger, material they would have lost eventually anyway, and, to compensate, they were gaining a little, usually a lot faster than if they'd had to rely on their own resources alone. This being the case, why bother too much about tracking Schnellinger down? A rough status quo was the most any intelligence service could hope for and a neutral organization fitted well enough into the overall scene. Until some genius in Washington had stuck his oar in, that is.

To be fair, the Americans had had their eyes half-open. They'd realized the Russians and Chinese weren't likely to appreciate the move and that, as a result, the duration of Schnellinger's usefulness to them would be strictly limited. What they hadn't banked on was the reaction of their faithful, Western allies, mistakenly assuming we'd all be delighted with American cunning. Of course, I could only speak for the British, but it was a fair bet the sentiments were the same in Bonn and Paris. And Tokyo, for all I knew. What few secrets we were allowed to have we liked to keep, even from lovable Uncle Sam. At first there'd merely been subdued muttering around Whitehall, but when Schnellinger had ordered Klemper, his chief hatchet man, to abduct Roger Brookes, action had been substituted for words. In so far as there were any rules to the game it was understood that men of Brooke's stature were sacrosanct.

At this point my reflections were interrupted by the realization that I'd kept Pawson waiting long enough. Accordingly I dropped the newspaper into the wastepaper basket, checked my youthful good looks in the mirror, and then strolled upstairs to pay my respects to the great white chief. Anne Lorrimer, Pawson's personal secretary, was in the outer office, wearing her usual tweedy office outfit which gave most people the impression she was butch. I knew better and returned her smile, deciding on the spur of the moment to invite her to cook dinner for me.

My unheralded entrance took Pawson by surprise and I caught him off guard, the central heating full on and the windows wide open. It was high time he gave up, I'd told him, but it remained his pet obsession, a strange flaw in his character. 'A form of relaxation' was the way Pawson himself put it. Unfortunately for his peace of mind there weren't many pigeons left in the Home Counties who didn't know that if they touched the bread crumbs sprinkled liberally on the windowsill they'd either be poisoned or have some maniac blasting away at them with an air pistol. The pigeons' answer was to fly over the building and crap on it from a great height.

When he heard me come into the office, Pawson swiveled round, slightly shamefaced, put the Webley into a drawer and told me to sit down. For a second or two he said nothing more, examining me carefully while I stared back at him. To be fair, he hadn't changed at all since we'd first met. His military mustache was trimmed with the same mathematical precision, his well-tended gray hair showed no signs of thinning, his blue eyes were as piercing as ever, his skin retained its habitual sun-lamp tan, and he was still chickening out of the surgery needed to straighten his nose. In fact, he displayed all the outward indications of being a second Dorian Gray and, knowing him for what he was, I was glad he'd never presented me with the portrait. Undoubtedly Pawson was thinking similar, charitable thoughts about me. The department thrived on mutual respect.

'You shouldn't blame yourself, Philis,' Pawson began

abruptly. 'What happened to Tracey wasn't your fault.'

It was a line I'd heard somewhere before. If enough people repeated it to me I'd end up with a sizable guilt complex.

'Thanks a lot,' I said acidly. 'You've taken a great weight off my mind. Perhaps you ought to know I don't blame myself either. The way I remember it, I wasn't the one who had the damn-fool idea of sending Tracey after Klemper in the first place.'

Pawson did his best to appear taken aback by my vehemence, but secretly he was probably pleased with the answer — the day I tipped my forelock to him would be the day he removed me from the active list. If the truth were known, it might even amuse Pawson to have a subordinate who refused to subordinate himself. My attitude was much simpler, based on the premise that I hadn't applied for a job with SR(2), I'd been press-ganged into it. Although I worked for Pawson, I could see no reason to lick his feet, or any other part of his anatomy come to that, and Pawson appreciated my spirit. This was why I received all the dirtiest assignments.

'You seemed rather conscience-stricken yesterday,' Pawson commented, retaining the same mild tone.

'Horror-stricken is nearer the mark,' I answered. 'It's high time somebody taught Schnellinger the rules. Since the Americans took him under their wing he seems to think he's God Almighty.'

'I'd say yesterday was an instructive start to his education,' Pawson came back, 'and it won't end there. After what happened to Tracey we're authorized to go the whole hog, regardless of protests from Washington.'

This was news to me. Welcome news, I might add.

'Collins told me Tracey managed to pass on something

before he died,' Pawson continued. 'Was it important?'

'It must have been to him. He gave me a name.'

'Whose name?'

Pawson was leaning forward in his seat, the greatest display of excitement he ever allowed himself, the equivalent of a war dance by anyone else. He didn't like his agents being killed, regarding such acts as personal insults.

'Sutters,' I said bluntly, interested to see his reaction.

Initially Pawson sank back in his chair to gaze at the ceiling, repeating the name under his breath. Although his face remained impassive I knew a lot of high-powered thinking was taking place in the devious labyrinths of his mind, and I didn't begrudge him the three or four minutes he spent silent. The previous day I'd taken the same number of hours to work it out, which helped to explain why Pawson headed the department and I'd only just aspired to a broom cupboard of an office.

'Tracey must have bumped into the Russians somewhere along the line,' Pawson announced when he had everything in order.

'That's certainly what it looks like.'

As a reward Pawson shot me a startled glance. He'd never fully accepted the idea of my possessing a brain.

'You've heard of Sutters, then?'

'Of course I have,' I said virtuously. 'When I initial a file it means I've read it. In any case, I know him personally, not just from a sheet of paper.'

This time Pawson frowned, a trifle uncertainly because he wasn't sure how serious I was. If you worked for a branch, or twig, of British intelligence, fraternization with known Soviet agents wasn't encouraged.

'How personally?' he asked suspiciously.

'We see each other once or twice a month,' I confessed. 'We get on well together.'

Although I'd twisted the knife, the outcome of a brief mental struggle was that Pawson decided to drop the matter. Evidently he agreed with me and thought the contact might prove useful. I lit a cigarette while Pawson settled down to more brainwork.

'Now why would Tracey use his dying breath to name a Russian agent?' he mused.

The question was meant to be rhetorical but, as I had the answer, I thought I might as well step in.

'It's pretty obvious.' My voice was casual, hours of painful thought concealed behind the nonchalance. 'As you implied, the Russians are gunning for Schnellinger. They're like us. While Schnellinger was neutral they used him, along with everyone else. Now the Americans have bought him they regard him as a menace. I'd say Sutters is the KGB's man on the job, Tracey's counterpart.'

'Any other thoughts on the matter?'

Since I'd chosen to be clever, Pawson was drawing in the noose. Around my neck.

'Plenty,' I told him. 'We could save a lot of time and money, not to mention prevent bad feeling with the CIA, by leaving the Russians to do our dirty work for us. The only fly in the ointment is Brookes. We can't afford to have him fall into the hands of the Russians. It'll be bad enough if he opens his heart to the Americans.'

'So?' Pawson prompted.

The rope was almost touching my neck, the time to stop showing off and to make a strategic withdrawal.

'The rest is more your line of country, sir,' I said servilely.

Showing Pawson I was on the ball was one thing, but the day I carried the can for him was a long, long way off. Fully aware of my motives, Pawson was laughing on the far side of the desk, genuinely amused, and I smiled back. It was at moments like this that we understood why we put up with each other.

'You defer to my greater experience?' Pawson suggested, still smiling.

'Something like that,' I agreed.

'O.K., we'll have Sutters brought in. As you're a friend of his, you'd better think of some scheme to lure him away from his house tonight.'

'There's no need. It's his night for woodwork.' Pawson was looking a trifle blank and I thought I'd better explain myself. 'He goes to one of the local technical colleges once a week — he's making a table or something. The house should be empty for at least a couple of hours.'

'You're sure?'

'Positive.'

'Fine. I'll send the stuff down to you this afternoon.'

'What stuff?' I asked, deliberately being stupid.

This was for the benefit of the unseen tape recorder. If anything should go wrong I wanted the blame placed squarely at the right door.

'The microfilm you're going to plant at his house to-night,' Pawson explained patiently. 'He's hardly likely to leave any of his own lying around.'

The interview was over and I was about to go when I remembered my plans for Anne Lorrimer. A quiet dinner might still be salvaged.

'Is it O.K. if I requisition one of the secretaries for the evening?' I asked from the door. 'If I'm going to spend three or four hours sitting in a parked car it'll look less suspicious if I have company.'

Pawson considered my request for a moment, then perked up visibly.

'I can't see why not,' he said, barely able to suppress his evil grin. 'Take Miss Sherwood. It's high time she did a spot of field work.'

It was on the tip of my tongue to tell Pawson I thought she'd worked in fields, haystacks, car back seats and anything else that was handy, but I held the remark back. Now I was positive. The old bastard did know I knew she was his niece.

Tel Aviv, Israel, January 1972

General Brinkmann savored the view from the balcony with the same intensity as when he'd first seen it, back in 1946. Then he had been a penniless, illegal immigrant, someone who had clawed his way to the Promised Land from a central European ghetto, a graduate of Dachau. Now, outside of the Knesset or the regular armed services, he was one of the most powerful men in the country. The knowledge gave him no sense of satisfaction, just an overbearing awareness of responsibility.

Behind him he heard Miteck toss the file onto the desk, and Brinkmann turned round to face the room, momentarily blind from the bright sunshine outside.

'Well, Jan,' he said. 'Does that satisfy you?'

'Klemper escaped,' Miteck pointed out. 'He's still alive.'

'He won't be for long. The British want to find Schnellinger, and Klemper is the only person who can tell them his identity. Besides, even if they're not primarily interested in Klemper himself, he signed his own death warrant when he had that British agent killed.'

'I only hope you're right.'

It was not a strong objection. After so many years, a month or two more was of no importance. Nor did it matter whose hands performed the execution, only that it should take place. Miteck had made arrangements of his own to insure that it did, arrangements of which Brinkmann was unaware.

'How's your daughter?' Brinkmann asked, changing the subject. 'It's a long while since I last saw her.'

'Maria's as healthy as ever,' Miteck answered. 'At the moment she's on holiday.'

For the life of him the General couldn't understand the reason for Miteck's smile.

2

JOHN SUTTERS hadn't been born until the age of twenty-five and his birth had coincided with the death of Nikolai Kuznets, the son of a Magnitogorsk steelworker. The KGB scouting system had spotted young Nikolai shortly after his twelfth birthday, noting his above average intelligence, his natural aptitude for languages, and his athletic prowess. This initial survey had marked him as promising material, an assessment which regular reports on other aspects of his character had done nothing to disprove, and at the age of sixteen Nikolai had been spirited away to the big KGB training school near Krasnoyarsk. When he had eventually resurfaced, it had been in London under the new name of John Sutters.

By the time I'd made Sutters's acquaintance he was already an important man, an aristocrat in the intelligence world. For a start he was semiautonomous, as independent as anyone who worked for the Russians could be. His base was in London, the place where he ran a small, perfectly legitimate import and export company which specialized in trade with countries on the far side of the Iron Curtain, and which earned more than enough to maintain his discreetly expensive house in Stanmore. We knew a considerable amount about his activities, largely by piecing together isolated snippets of information, and had no reason at all for pulling him in. What he chose to do in the satellite countries was none of our business and he'd never done anything remotely illegal in the United Kingdom. This was why I had to visit his house to plant evidence calculated to convince Special Branch that Sutters had started collecting British military secrets. What such an act was likely to do to our friendship I didn't know, but at least it would keep Pawson happy.

By a quarter past seven my newly acquired Mini Cooper was parked in the shadow between two streetlamps, less than half a mile from where Sutters lived. Miss Sherwood was beside me, her subtle harem perfume filling the car, and I was glad there was no bench front seat to tempt me.

'What do we do now?' she asked hopefully.

If it had been what she was thinking we'd have been in court on a lewd vagrancy charge in the morning.

'You snuggle up close and I put my arm round you,' I told her.

'Now what?' she prompted, once she'd done her best to join me inside my topcoat.

'We talk. Discuss the weather or something.'

'Is that all?'

Disappointment mingled with a sense of outrage in her voice.

'It is,' I assured her.

She drew away slightly, examining my face in the dim light, unable to understand my lack of initiative. Unexpectedly she laughed.

'I think you're afraid of Uncle Charles,' she taunted.

Half an hour later, when Sutters's Jaguar came into sight, I was more than ready for a breath of fresh air. As soon as his rear lights had disappeared I flipped on my two-way radio.

'He's left,' I said.

'Right,' Soames responded. 'I'm ready.'

To fill in time I busied myself scraping off lipstick from the lower half of my face, watched by Miss Sherwood, who had sunk decorously back into the corner of her seat, displaying her legs up to the navel. Despite the blatant exhibitionism, I didn't hold it against her. They were the sort of legs every woman would like to be able to show off, and there was nothing much wrong with her navel.

'I've got him,' Soames announced a couple of minutes later. 'I'll let you know if anything goes wrong.'

Stiffly I clambered from the car and walked round the corner into Methuen Avenue. There was nobody else about, which was hardly surprising considering the temperature. Everyone with any sense was in front of a fire not out housebreaking, and that's where I would have liked to have been as well.

Even with Sutters safely off the premises, the prospect of my evening's work didn't exactly thrill me to the marrow. Getting into the house was no problem as I had a key. It was what happened afterward that worried me. The only reason Sutters didn't bother with alarms was the friendly little pooch he kept as a pet, a ruddy great Alsatian called Wolf. Judging purely by the size of its teeth, it would be a tossup between the dog and a shoal of hungry piranhas as to who could strip a man down to the bone faster.

Although I had been introduced to the beast several times, had even stroked it tentatively, I wasn't too sure Wolf would recognize me as a friend. If he didn't there were likely to be some fun and games, ending up with Wolf enjoying a good, nourishing meal. To make matters worse, and quite apart from the risk of bringing the RSPCA down on my neck, I couldn't afford to maltreat the poor animal. McAllister of Special Branch might only use his head for growing dandruff, but the chances were he might be a trifle suspicious if he discovered a slaughtered dog lying on Sutters's living room carpet, especially after the anonymous tip he was due to receive in an hour's time.

On the doorstep I stopped for a minute, partly to make sure nobody was watching me, partly to convince myself I wasn't really scared stiff. It wouldn't do to let Wolf know I was crapping bricks. After a few deep breaths I unlocked the door, going into the dark hall fast. Immediately I was greeted by a hostile growl, coming from my right and above. No sooner had I worked out that the dog must be on the stairs than I heard its paws coming toward me.

'Stay, Wolf,' I said firmly.

He stopped, evidently remembering either my smell or voice. Just the same, he hadn't lost his growl and didn't sound at all friendly. By the light filtering through the hall window I could see his outline at the foot of the stairs, crouched ready to spring, not really sure whether I should be in the house or not. He could remember his master introducing me as a friend but this conflicted with his basic training of ripping out intruders' throats. My throat was fine as it was and I decided to press the friendship angle. Hunkering down on my haunches left me in a lousy defensive position if Wolf did attack, but it couldn't possibly be construed as a hostile move, even by a dumb animal.

'Here, boy,' I said, extending the shaking hand of friendship.

Wolf crouched lower, his belly touching the ground, the

growl becoming a rumble at the back of his throat. It returned fast when I put my hand in my pocket to pull out the steak I'd brought him.

'Come on, Wolf,' I coaxed. 'You know me.'

After a second's hesitation the dog began snaking forward on its belly, heading for the meat I'd pushed in front of me. Although he hadn't accepted me yet, the food definitely had him interested. One baleful eye fixed on me, he sniffed it carefully, then greedily gulped it down in two mouthfuls. Thankfully I straightened up, taking the weight from my creaking bones.

'Time for beddy-byes, Baskerville,' I told the brute.

Suddenly Wolf decided I wasn't a friend, his hind-quarters tensing as he prepared to leap, until his legs went weak beneath him and he stood there stupidly, struggling to retain his balance. The effort was too much for him and gracefully, in slow motion, the animal collapsed to the floor, continuing to growl throatily even after sleep had overcome him.

Relieved, I expelled my breath in a noisy sigh and wiped the sweat from my forehead. The drug was guaranteed for at least a quarter of an hour, plenty of time for what I had to do. The sole remaining problem was to put the micro-film somewhere it wouldn't look too much like a plant, yet where it wasn't likely to be overlooked. It took a little over a minute to whip off the back of the television set in the living room and tape the small metal container inside. Of course, it was an insult to Sutters's intelligence to suppose he'd use such an obvious hiding place — come to that he'd never have kept incriminating evidence overnight — but I had to remember I was catering for a Special Branch search party. The old saw about finding a needle in a haystack didn't apply to them. They'd have a job finding the hay-stack.

Petrov was far too strong for me. He was a man built on a monumental scale, six feet five inches tall with a massive, muscular frame to go with the height. At the top, if you risked a crick in the neck by looking up that far, he sported an extravagant beard in the Cossack tradition, the luxuriant growth tinged with gray although he'd only just turned forty. Not that his appearance had anything to do with his tennis, only his size. The wooden surface at the club was ideally suited to his serve and volley game and the ease with which he took the first set made a mockery of the 6–4 scoreline. Belatedly realizing I couldn't match him at his own game, I changed tactics, certain that while the brute strength might be on the far side of the net he couldn't match me for artistry and skill. I began chipping my return of serve low over the net, then hoisting top-spin lobs to the baseline. On my service I concentrated on his weaker backhand and no longer went for outright winners on the first volley. Needless to say, he won the second set 6–1.

'Let's double bets and make it the best of five,' I suggested, reluctant to concede defeat.

'O.K., Philis,' Petrov agreed. 'I don't mind taking your money.'

Changing tactics yet again, I adopted an even more defensive game, remaining on the baseline and concentrating exclusively on spinning out the rallies. As the set progressed, Petrov flagged visibly, the gallons of vodka he must have consumed at embassy receptions gradually taking their toll. My superior physical fitness was the deciding factor and I, at last, broke serve to win the set at 9–7. From then on it was easy.

'Who said the West was decadent?' I sneered sportingly as I accepted two five-pound notes in the dressing room.

Petrov said something unpleasant in Russian and patted me playfully on the shoulder. After he'd helped me up from the bench, he set off for the showers, an opportunity for me to admire the two puckered scars on his back. They meant someone must have gunned him from behind, because Petrov wasn't the type of man to run away. Ten years before, he'd been one of the top Soviet agents in the field; recently he'd been upgraded and given a desk job at the London embassy. Officially, of course, he figured on the list as one of the military attachés. In fact he was coordinator for the entire Russian intelligence network in Britain.

Our ablutions completed, we made our way to a dark corner of the bar upstairs. It was the middle of the afternoon and we were the only occupants apart from the steward.

'Well, Philis,' he said once we were settled. 'What can I do for you? If you want to defect I can have you out of the country inside twenty-four hours.'

In reply I shook my head, treating him to a friendly smile at the same time.

'Not likely,' I told him. 'You don't pay enough and I've heard all about those Russian winters. I was thinking more along the lines of a friendly discussion about John Sutters.'

It was Petrov's turn to smile, his gray eyes twinkling with amusement.

'John Sutters?' he said. 'Who's he?'

'Be serious,' I rejoindered. 'In case you're worried, this conversation is strictly off the record.'

Petrov settled his bulky frame more comfortably in the wicker chair, brought out a flat, metal box the size and shape of a cigarette case, placed it on the table between us, and pressed a switch on the side. It was considerably more advanced than anything we'd produced. Even by straining my ears to the limit I couldn't detect the slightest hum.

'Typical,' I commented. 'I go to the trouble of embedding a transmitter in my navel and you have to ruin reception with that gadget.'

The Russian shrugged his shoulders.

'You work for Pawson,' he stated, as though this was an adequate explanation. His smile returned as something occurred to him. 'I might condescend to play tennis with you, but you're still a degenerate, neofascist lackey of capitalist imperialism.'

He pronounced the words with relish.

'Did you make that up yourself, or have you been reading *Pravda* again?' I asked, unimpressed by the dialectic. 'Anyway, now you've got the compliments off your chest, can we talk about Sutters?'

Petrov produced a long, black Cuban cheroot and lit it contemplatively. He was still trying to work out what I was after, worried about being one step behind the game.

'I honestly don't know what there is to discuss,' he said deliberately. 'Sutters was completely independent, I've never even met the man. In fact, it was quite a surprise to hear he'd been arrested because, to the best of my knowledge, he's never been operational in this country. He must have been up to something behind my back, a rather disturbing situation.'

His train of thought amused me. So far it hadn't occurred to him that Sutters had been framed. Petrov suspected Moscow had passed him by, given Sutters an assignment in England about which he knew nothing. If this really had been the case it would have meant Petrov's superiors in the Kremlin had lost faith in him, his post as coordinator had been placed in jeopardy. I thought it would be a friendly gesture to put him out of his misery.

'Don't upset yourself,' I told him. 'Moscow isn't stabbing you in the back. The arrest was stage-managed by Pawson. All the evidence Special Branch is so excited about was planted by me.'

Silence fell, the only sound the swish of the steward's cloth on the bar top. From the way Petrov was staring at the glowing end of his cheroot I realized he was settling down to some hard thinking, a chance for me to collect two more beers. When I returned with the replenished glasses he was still deep in thought and I let him be. He had to be good to hold down his present position. Just how good he was would be shown by his conclusions.

'It has to be connected with Schnellinger,' Petrov said at last, a great weight lifting from his brow. 'I fail to see how it fits but it can't possibly be anything else.'

Impressed, I gave him an enthusiastic clap, making the steward throw a startled glance in our direction. With men like Petrov at the top it was no wonder the Russians knew more of our secrets than we did ourselves.

'Right first time,' I told him. 'To put it in a nutshell, you want Sutters and would like to see Schnellinger out of business. We don't particularly want Sutters and we feel the same way as you about Schnellinger. That's all there is to it.'

Petrov raised his eyebrows.

'Aren't your American friends likely to raise some objections?'

'We weren't thinking of telling them,' I answered. 'In any case, they've only themselves to blame. Having an efficient, nonpartisan intelligence outfit on the go was to everyone's advantage, but the Americans never could leave a good thing alone. With Schnellinger in their pocket they're rocking the boat.'

'I couldn't agree more. Exactly what is Pawson thinking of?'

Hunching forward over my drink, I began to tell him. There was a lot to say and, apart from Petrov's occasional grunt or interjection, I held the floor for the best part of half an hour. When I'd finished, the Russian was more or less in complete agreement with Pawson's proposition, and so he should have been, because it was to the advantage of both of us. With business over, Petrov didn't hang round for any protracted social chitchat, knowing he had a lot of ciphered cables to dispatch. He drained his beer, rose to his feet, and proffered an outsize hand. I accepted it, regretting the action almost immediately as I winced at the strength of his grip.

'When this is over you must let me have my revenge at tennis,' he suggested.

'I'm afraid it's not on, in England at any rate,' I said with genuine regret. It wasn't every day I won £10.

'Why not?' Petrov asked, surprised. 'Don't you enjoy my company?'

'It's not that,' I hastened to explain, 'but as from today you're no longer persona grata in the United Kingdom. We're asking the embassy to have you out of the country inside a fortnight.'

Petrov shot me a sharp glance, saw I was serious and, after a momentary pause, came out with a thunderclap of a laugh.

'Philis,' he said, 'I like you a lot, but one of these days you'll have to be taken down a peg or two.'

Although I joined in the laughter I didn't find his re-mark as funny as all that. He was just as serious as I'd been about his deportation.

Before leaving the club I allowed Petrov half an hour's lead, availing myself of another drink in the meantime. As a concession to discretion it was a dead loss, the lads from DI5 picking me up less than a hundred yards down the street. The first I knew of it was when the Rover pulled in to the curb beside me and the rear door opened.

'Inside,' Joyce ordered.

Looking at his smarmy young face in the dark interior of the car, I laughed. He was so inept I might just as well have wept.

'Get stuffed,' I told him, turning my back.

The Rover kept pace with me as I walked along the street. Inside Joyce was making frantic gestures, even let-ting me see his gun, and I was losing my temper. The idiot was so incompetent he was likely to do something stupid, even by his standards. Luckily there was a phone booth on the corner.

'Great news,' I told Pawson. 'It's Joyce's day for keeping tabs on Petrov.'

Pawson didn't say anything but I distinctly heard his smothered groan.

'The lunatic wants to take me in for questioning,' I went on. 'He's even waving a gun round.'

Pawson groaned again.

'Where is he now?' he asked.

'Just outside the phone booth. From the look of him he's on musth.'

'You'd better go with him,' Pawson decided. 'We don't

want a regrettable incident in the street. I'll phone Henry and make sure you're not detained.'

'Fix it fast,' I advised him. 'If Joyce tries to throw his weight round there's likely to be trouble.'

The receiver went down with a satisfactory bang, then I stepped out of the booth. As I'd told Pawson, Joyce was hovering round on the pavement, with what he fondly fancied to be a snarl fixed on his lips. To me it looked more as though he'd sat on something which had gone right up but I was prejudiced. None too gently Joyce jabbed his gun into my midriff, prejudicing me some more.

'Let's go,' he said, steering me toward the back seat of the Rover.

Evidently Pawson hadn't taken my advice about contacting Henry Tate quickly because I was led straight to an inter-rogation room. Once there I sat myself on a hard, straight-backed chair, fed up to the back teeth, and lit a cigarette. Joyce promptly knocked it from my mouth, not quite enough provocation for what I felt like doing to him. Satis-fied in his own mind that he'd established command, Joyce perched precariously on a corner of the desk and treated me to his version of a steely glare. Kramer, the man who'd driven the car, leant comfortably against the doorjamb and waited for me finally to lose my temper. I yawned dis-creetly to show how impressed I was.

'You were with Petrov,' Joyce accused. 'What did you talk about?'

'I would have thought that was obvious. We were plot-ting to assassinate the Cabinet, George Best and the entire Royal Family.'

Apparently Joyce wasn't quite the idiot I thought him to be, because he guessed I might not be telling the truth. For a moment he seemed to be on the verge of hitting me but he didn't. Instead he contented himself with an angry flush and did his best to ignore my reply.

'All right, Philis,' he growled. 'We'll leave that for the moment. Who did you phone after you left the club?'

'The Good Samaritans,' I told him. 'When I realized DI five was still employing a prick like you I felt like committing suicide. They told me to pretend you were only a bad dream.'

This time Joyce did try to hit me, the excuse I'd been waiting for. Moving my head out of the way of his fist, I grabbed hold of his lapels, pulled him forward and butted him hard with my ascending head. Joyce's nose spread redly across his face, more than justifying his anguished yelp. So that he wouldn't concentrate exclusively on the pain in his nose, I dragged him off the desk and threw him against the wall, hitting him the odd inch or two below the belt to stop him bouncing back and loosening his teeth with my knee when he bent over. While the Marquess of Queensberry might not have approved, Joyce had never waved a gun under his lordship's nose.

The DI5 man lay on the floor, alternately moaning and spitting out blood, doing so without any sympathy from me. He deserved to be hurt. If I'd tried anything so corny on anyone else in the building I would've been a hospital case.

Kramer was still over by the door, making no effort to hide his pleasure, and, much as I appreciated his attitude, this worried me. He'd no seniority worth talking about and it was hardly his fault he had Joyce as a nominal superior. It was on the tip of my tongue to suggest he do something to restrain me when the matter was taken out of my hands, the door opening to admit Henry Tate. He was a balding, mild-faced little man only a month away from retirement, his eyes looking perpetually surprised behind the thin-rimmed glasses. Before he spoke he shortsightedly examined the moaning Joyce, his eyes becoming a bit more surprised, the corners of his mouth quirking up fractionally. His examination completed, he turned to me.

'I'm sorry about the inconvenience, Philis,' he said, seeming to think the writhing body on the floor was a matter of no importance. 'Perhaps a drink might make you feel better disposed toward us.'

This was my kind of speech and I followed him out of the room, pretending not to notice Kramer's congratulatory wink. Upstairs, in Tate's inner sanctum, I was seated in a comfortable leather chair with a whisky for company. In return for the hospitality I felt I owed some kind of apology.

'I hope you don't think I damaged Joyce for pleasure,' I told Tate. 'He really was behaving like an imbecile.'

'Think nothing of it,' Tate said expansively. 'The lesson might even do him some good.'

I shrugged my shoulders helplessly. The entire episode was beyond my understanding.

'Why on earth don't you get rid of him?' I asked. 'He'll never amount to anything.'

'I know, I know,' Tate agreed, 'but Joyce does have one priceless asset.'

'What's that?' I inquired incredulously.

As far as I was concerned Joyce could walk and talk and that was the limit of his usefulness.

'He's totally expendable,' Tate answered gently. 'There aren't many men you could say that about.'

Belatedly I wished I hadn't been quite so rough with

Joyce. There had been a time when Pawson had echoed Tate's sentiments, only he'd been thinking of me.

London, England, January 1972

The austere, antiseptic prison cell was no home, sweet home, but it did represent a welcome haven after the uninterrupted hours of meaningless interrogation. Above all, it offered Sutters an opportunity to put his thoughts in order, the first lull in a kaleidoscopic rush of events. So far, he knew that somebody had gone to considerable trouble to frame him, otherwise he was completely in the dark. To begin with, there had been the late-night invasion of his home, the search warrant waved under his nose, vague mention of information received, several pairs of outsize feet ruining his carpets, ecstatic shouts of 'Eureka' from his living room. This last had initiated the second phase, the change of venue, the standard bright light dazzling his eyes and the interminable hours of questioning, totally unproductive although it had resulted in his being charged. Now, lying full length on the narrow bed, a lumpy contraption specifically designed for masochistic misogynists, Sutters was able to express his carefully nurtured grudge.

'Philis,' he said out loud, addressing a crack in the ceiling. 'That two-faced bastard Philis.'

Nevertheless, despite his anger and uncertainty, Sutters managed to smile, a trifle bitterly. If he ever appeared in court he intended to make sure he had company in the dock.

3

THE YOUTH BLEW SMOKE in my face and said something
unprintable. Inwardly I sighed. After five sets with Petrov
I was feeling stiff, definitely not in the mood for any more
exercise. Unfortunately I wasn't likely to receive a civil
answer without slapping him round, especially as his girl
friend was watching. He wasn't a particularly inspiring
sight with his acne, lank, greasy hair, scruffy jeans and dirty
leather jacket. To round off the repulsive picture his
mouth hung slackly open, neatly framing the strand of
tobacco stuck to his top lip, and he certainly wasn't worthy
of his companion. Even a touch of jealousy didn't make
me more disposed to hit him, not when I'd already beaten
up my man for the day.

'All I want to do is talk to him,' I explained briefly.

Again he replied with something unprintable, a different
word this time. It still didn't add to my vocabulary, so,
regretfully, I removed the strand of tobacco from his lip
with my fist. I didn't hit him too hard because we had the
full routine to go through. He had to bring out the knife
from his jacket pocket to show how tough he was, I had
to take it away from him to prove I was a little bit tougher,
then we could try again.

The edge of the switchblade glittered evilly in his hand
when he pushed himself up from the floor, making it some-

thing of a relief to discover he didn't know how to use it. There was nothing much wrong with his preliminary weaving — he'd seen this enough times on television; he just didn't have the slightest idea how to set about sticking the knife into me. On his first lunge I took it away from him, slapping him back onto the sofa, where he held his bruised face in his hands and began to snivel. I sat on the arm of a chair, waiting for him to snap out of it.

'I can tell you where to find Evans,' the girl said, proving she could speak.

The voice matched her looks, which made her relationship with the specimen on the sofa all the more puzzling. She was only twenty or so but she epitomized all the better features of modern youth — long, slender legs, flat stomach and buttocks, pleasantly taut little breasts, big, innocent eyes and a slight twist of the mouth to indicate the innocence shouldn't be taken for granted. With all this I could even forgive her close-cropped blond hair.

'You didn't think to mention it earlier,' I noted. 'Or perhaps you enjoyed watching me knock your boy friend around.'

She shrugged indifferently, emphasizing the fact that there was no brassiere under the sweater. Her jeans were tight enough to show there wasn't much beneath them either.

'It wasn't any of my business,' she stated.

'So what made you change your mind?'

'Well, I can't stay here now, can I, so I'll take you to see Evans. I hope you've a car.'

The line of reasoning was way beyond me but I let it pass. Her personal philosophy was of no importance; Bill Evans was. The Mini was outside and after I'd escorted her

down to it I had a careful look round. Although the man
Tate had had tailing me was unlikely to have found me
again, I had to make sure. Five minutes' driving with an
eye on the mirror reassured me and I began responding to
the girl's directions. We ended up on the Isle of Dogs, in a
deserted side street flanked by desolate warehouses. The
one she indicated appeared to be as godforsaken as all the
others.

'Go up the outside stairs and through the door at the
top,' she directed. 'You'll find Evans inside.'

'Aren't you coming with me?'

The girl shook her head disgustedly. 'I'll wait in the car.'

As long as she'd brought me to the right place I didn't
give a damn one way or the other and I took her at her
word, but the ignition keys went with me. At the foot of
the stairs, my coat collar turned up against the foggy chill, I
could hear faint sounds of music above the volume increased inexorably the farther I went up the rickety worm-
eaten steps. Inside the door I was hit simultaneously by
the waves of noise and smoke, a lot of the latter coming
from cigarettes you couldn't buy across the counter, and it
took my eyes a few seconds to adjust to the fug. When they
had, I decided they needn't have bothered because func-
tional was a word which would have flattered the social
club. There was a juke box in the far corner, a ramshackle
bar to one side and a haphazard splattering of tables and
chairs. Apart from these there were warped floorboards,
brick walls and assorted cobwebs tastefully arranged in the
rafters. Considering the room was almost the size of Wem-
bley Stadium, with the Empire Pool, thrown in, it wasn't
exactly overfurnished.

Even so, it was far too good for the occupants and, look-

ing them over, I seriously considered the possibility of
Pawson having made a mistake. There were about fifty
people in the club, all of them seated barring one lone
couple, hopped up to the eyeballs, who were either dancing
or having it away. With all the smoke it was hard to tell.
Of the customers no more than a dozen were female, most
of them too young to be full-blown pros, just rank scrub-
bers or enthusiastic sham amateurs. The majority of the
males were in the same age group — late teens or early
twenties — and they had one other thing in common.
They were, without exception, staring at me, making no
effort to mask their hostility. It must have been a long
while since they last saw somebody who regarded washing
and shaving as an integral part of life.

'What do you want?'

This from a youth at the nearest table, thumbs hooked
belligerently in his belt. The blare from the juke box had
stopped a second or two before, the room silent while I was
scutinized, and the words must have carried to everyone.

'I'm looking for Bill Evans,' I explained, on my very best
behavior.

'He's looking for Bill Evans,' the comedian repeated to
the room at large, an air of wonder in his voice.

For some reason the sophisticated parody had everybody
in the club rocking with laughter. Apart from me, that is.
I was quietly developing a pain in the coccyx region.

'Can you tell me where I can find him?' I asked, still
doing my best to remain civil.

'Try asking at the bar,' the yob suggested, his smirk
widening.

A moment later the reason became apparent. As I
walked past he stuck a foot between my legs and I found

myself examining the dusty floorboards at ground level.
On this occasion the general hilarity nearly brought the
roof down. Determined to keep my temper, I stayed on the
floor while I slowly counted up to ten, proud of the fact I
didn't have to use my fingers, then levered myself back onto
my feet. Laughing Boy had his head thrown back, mouth
wide open as he guffawed uncontrollably. When the cold
metal of the Colt went between his decaying molars he
sobered up fast, eyes bugging as he realized his mistake.
The rest weren't long in following suit. I might be an old
fuddy-duddy in his thirties but the gun did help to bridge
the generation gap.

'I didn't think that was funny,' I announced.

Although I had spoken quietly I didn't doubt that everyone in the room had heard me. They were all thinking of
what would happen if I pulled the trigger, especially
Laughing Boy, who had the most to lose. Like his head.

'What the hell is going on in here?'

The question shattered the tension with one blow, the
relaxation so palpable it filled the club. Everybody turned
toward the source of the interruption, toward the man
standing in a doorway at the far end of the room, one arm
slung casually round the shoulders of an attractive brunette
in a see-through shift. Evans himself was in his middle
thirties, a short curly-haired barrel of a man, only a little
over five and a half feet tall with the shoulders of a heavy-
weight. As nobody else seemed inclined to answer him I
appointed myself spokesman.

'We're having a lesson in social etiquette,' I explained
without moving the gun. 'An informal discussion about the
finer points of good manners and decorum.'

Evans took his arm from round the brunette's neck,
patted her affectionately on the rump, and came forward

into the club, taking in the situation as he walked. When he was closer I could see his face was an aggregation of bumps and angles, an attractive-ugly face, the dark eyes displaying unmistakable signs of intelligence. He came to a half a foot or two away from me.

'Rob been giving you trouble, has he?' he asked, with only the faintest trace of a Welsh lilt.

'Not really,' I replied. 'We don't seem to share the same sense of humor, that's all.'

Evans sucked his teeth and nodded thoughtfully.

'You can put the gun away,' he said. 'You won't be needing it.'

Surprisingly the girl was still in the car when I eventually left Evans, almost blue with cold since she hadn't had the sense to bring a coat. Until we hit the Commercial Road I drove in silence, allowing her a chance to thaw out, the heater on full blast.

'Where to?' I asked as we headed back toward the City.

'Anywhere you like,' she answered indifferently. 'You're the driver.'

Briefly I concentrated on the road, braking to avoid a London Transport double-decker which had swung out dangerously in front of me. Leaning on the horn, I directed a few philosophic words at his exhaust. Just because their vehicles were bigger than anything else on the road some of the drivers thought they could get away with blue murder. One day I promised to buy myself a Chieftain tank and sort a few of the jokers out.

'Do you want to go back to your boy friend's place?' I asked, my emotions under control again.

'He's not my boy friend, for God's sake.' My question had insulted her. 'I only met him tonight.'

'Your place, then,' I suggested.

'I haven't got one,' she said helpfully.

Apparently she lived out of the small suitcase she'd thrown in the back.

'How about a hotel?'

'No money,' she answered succinctly.

Decisively I stopped fooling around, not wishing to become further involved in a conversation I couldn't hope to win, and headed for my flat, the girl beside me completely indifferent about our destination. Only when I parked the car did she display some signs of curiosity.

'Is this where you live?' she asked.

Instinctively I sensed something was wrong but for the life of me I couldn't work out what it was. For a minute I stood in the hall, endeavoring to pinpoint my unease, then decided I was becoming nervy in my old age.

'The living room is through there,' I informed the girl, indicating the door on the left. 'Make yourself comfortable while I brew some coffee.'

Three paces toward the kitchen I realized what had been bothering me. There were traces of Anne's perfume in the air and she hadn't been to the flat for four days, what might be called a natural break. Realization came too late for me to act upon it. Frozen in the hall, I watched the tragedy unfold in front of me. The girl switched on the living room light, there was a fifteen-second time lapse and Anne Lorrimer's voice came on the air.

'Hallo, Ph . . .' it started sleepily and tenderly.

There was an abrupt cutoff, a brief silence, then it returned in its icy, outraged form.

'Who the hell are you?' it demanded.

Leaden-footed, moving like an automaton, I headed

toward my Waterloo. Anne had been asleep on the sofa, curled up in front of the electric fire while she awaited my return. Now she was pulling on her shoes, her pinched nostrils and pale, strained features testifying to her feelings.

'It isn't what you're thinking, Anne.'

As I spoke I wondered how many thousands of men had come out with this excuse before me. The fact I was telling the truth didn't come into it. Anne ignored me completely, collecting her coat and handbag before she headed resolutely for the door. As she pushed past I grabbed her shoulder.

'Just listen for a minute —' I began.

This was as far as I got. Her right hand went back, the handbag blurred as it picked up speed and of a sudden I was shuddering from head to toe. Although my head didn't quite part company with my body it certainly wasn't through Anne's want of trying. With a crash which threatened to splinter the door she was gone.

Addressing the busts of Rasputin and de Sade on the mantelpiece, I delivered a brief monologue, decidedly profane in composition. Luckily they'd both heard it all before and didn't bat an eyelid. With this off my chest I was free to pay some attention to the girl who was standing by the wall, feeling repentant about the scene she'd provoked. One hand was over her mouth, her face was red and her eyes were popping from the effort of holding back her laughter. It was my night for meeting people with highly developed senses of humor.

'Your face,' she spluttered, tears trickling down her cheeks. 'You should have seen your face.'

'The spare bedroom is yours,' I said woodenly, wondering why I didn't kick her out into the street. 'You'll find bedclothes in the airing cupboard in the kitchen.'

On my way to visit Pawson the next morning, I didn't stop for a chat at Anne's desk as her normal, butch office look had acquired glacial overtones. Fortunately, she wasn't to know Julie was still residing at my flat, otherwise I'd probably have been dodging ashtrays.

'What have you been doing to my secretary?' Pawson inquired once the door was closed.

He paused to examine me more closely, then came up with another question.

'What's happened to your face?' he asked with considerable interest.

'Mr. Pawson, sir,' I said, rubbing my bruised cheek. 'I respectfully submit that my private life is none of your business.' Before he could think of a reply I pushed the expenses chit for £10 across the desk. 'Sign this, will you? Petrov insisted on playing for money.'

After another look at my cheek Pawson signed without raising any objections. Now it worked out at £4 a set. While this didn't put me in the Rod Laver bracket, at least it was a start.

'You found Evans all right, did you?'

'Yes, no problems,' I told him, preferring to gloss over the incidents of the previous night. 'It's arranged for the day after tomorrow.'

'How much?'

'It's on the Russians. Evans settled for five thousand, as I'm going to handle the difficult part.'

Pawson looked pleased with the news, just as he always did when he saved money.

'I suppose I won't be seeing much of you for a while,' he remarked, facing the prospect with commendable calm.

'Not if we stick to the agreement.'

'We abide by the terms,' Pawson said firmly. 'The Russians will play it straight, I'd bet on that. Once Sutters is out of prison you two are on your own. Unless, of course, you discover the job is too big for you to manage alone.'

I nodded in assent, the arrangement suiting me down to the ground. It would be a pleasure not to have Pawson breathing down my neck twenty-four hours a day and I shared his feeling about the Russians. Once they agreed to play ball they were a hell of a sight more trustworthy than some of our so-called allies.

'Have you decided what equipment you'll need from Stores?' Pawson inquired.

He accepted the sheet of paper, then ran down the list without comment until he reached the last item.

'What's this?' he demanded, genuinely shocked.

'The long word is bulletproof,' I said helpfully.

'For Christ's sake,' he went on, ignoring my reply. 'They're for VIP's only. I doubt whether I could lay my hands on one even if I wanted to.' My request had struck to the very core of Pawson's being. 'Have you any idea how much they cost?'

I wasn't in the mood for argument.

'Dead or alive, Roger Brookes has to be recovered, doesn't he?'

'It's absolutely essential,' Pawson agreed.

'Fine. And you've told me exactly what to do when, and if, Schnellinger has been dealt with?'

'I have.'

'Well, in that case, what do you think Moscow will instruct Sutters to do? I'm going to need one of those vests.'

Despite the cogency of my argument Pawson still vetoed

my request, just as I'd suspected he would. Although it wasn't among the points he raised, I knew he was thinking of the department's secret service image. He'd rather his agents stopped their bullets like men than take sensible precautions, like wearing lightweight, bulletproof vests under their normal clothing.

London, England, January 1972

Sutters yawned and stroked the stubble on his chin. He didn't need a mirror to know how bloodshot his eyes were.

'Ask me another,' he suggested.

'Give me time,' McAllister answered patiently. 'For the moment I merely want to know how the microfilms came to be inside your television set.'

'Check through your notes. You'll see I've already told you at least a hundred times.'

'Tell me again,' McAllister persisted. 'I always enjoy a good story.'

Evidently someone had once told the Special Branch man how tiny drops of water could wear away the mightiest of boulders, a gem of information which had left a lasting impression. This made for a boring life, although Sutters found it infinitely preferable to the rubber truncheon approach.

'It was a plant,' he explained yet again. 'Somebody must have broken into my house while I was out.'

'Of course,' McAllister agreed, positively oozing sarcasm. 'That explains why none of the windows were broken or any of the locks tampered with.' He gave Sutters a friendly smile. 'What was your guard dog doing, the one you're so proud of? Having a quiet snooze?'

'Perhaps whoever it was had some aniseed with him,' Sutters said curtly, struck on a sensitive spot.

Apparently McAllister's stint was over because he'd settled back in his chair and was lighting his pipe, yielding the floor to the second interrogator. His name was Jenkins and he'd been assigned the soft-sell role.

'Listen, Sutters,' he began persuasively, pushing a pack of cigarettes across the table. 'You're in trouble, thirty years' worth of trouble. No jury is going to believe this cock-and-bull story of yours because it just doesn't hold water. Why don't you face facts and do yourself some good? We have you cold but we haven't located the leak at Portrush. We will eventually but it will take time. Unless you help us.' Jenkins paused. 'Tell me everything you know, contacts, codes, drops, the lot, and I'll make sure your cooperation is mentioned at the trial. It could mean quite a few years of your life.'

'In other words, if I help you you'll help me.'

'That's the size of it,' Jenkins confirmed, surprised by Sutters's alacrity in taking the bait. 'I can't promise what the judge's sentence will be but I can guarantee my every assistance if you're sensible.

Sutters helped himself to a cigarette, accepted a light from Jenkins and gave the proposition some thought. After a minute or so he decided it was possible some people would bite on the mangy old carrot, if hard to believe. The glance the two policemen had exchanged showed they, at least, had high hopes. It seemed a pity to disappoint them.

'All right,' Sutters announced, reaching a decision after a further minute's deliberation. 'I'll tell you about my contact but I'm afraid it's rather difficult to describe him.'

'Do your best,' McAllister encouraged, scenting victory.

Still Sutters refused to commit himself, held back by a few lingering doubts.

'You really will put in a good word for me?' he asked.

'We will,' Jenkins promised warmly. 'Go ahead.'

'O.K.,' Sutters agreed, his mind made up. 'He's a man in his fifties, average height but heavily built. His hair is gray, the eyes I'm not sure about.'

'Surely you can do better than that,' McAllister said when Sutters stopped. 'So far your description could fit almost anyone, including Jenkins here.'

'I'm sorry,' Sutters apologized, filled with contrition. 'He's such an average person, that's the trouble. There is something about his face, though.' With an effort he searched for the appropriate words. 'He has an air of bene-volence, the face of somone you could trust.'

'No distinguishing features?' Jenkins asked, unim-pressed. 'Anything that makes him stand out?'

Sutters shook his head.

'How about clothes?'

'He seems to favor dark suits and he always has the same overcoat. One of those waterproofed Gannex affairs with a tweed lining.'

'Anything else?'

It was McAllister's turn.

'Yes, there is,' Sutters's voice was suddenly animated. 'He smokes a pipe and his name is Wilson.'

That should teach them to keep him up all night with their stupid questions.

4

IF I'D FELT UNCOMFORTABLE traipsing round the country-side as an imitation milkman, I felt considerably worse in full police uniform. The wig and glasses contributed to my general unease but I had a lot more on my mind than this. Nobody would give a damn if I chose to impersonate a milkman; get caught in police uniform and I was liable to have the book thrown at me, SR(2) agent or not. The police could be more than uncooperative when they discovered they were being used as a cat's-paw, the ordinary machinery of justice perverted in the interests of a man like Pawson.

The fact that nobody was paying undue attention as we drove past was no source of reassurance at all. There was no reason for the man in the street to notice anything suspicious, as our dress was correct to the last button and the Black Maria was the genuine article. The real test would come when we reached the prison and underwent the scrutiny of the warders. Already the prison's depressing bulk was in sight and I had at least one of every known species of butterfly fluttering about in my stomach. Evans took his eyes from the road to give me a critical glance.

'Feeling nervous?' he asked in a not unfriendly tone.

'Not really,' I lied.

'Don't worry,' he said reassuringly, not taken in by my denial. 'It should be a snip.'

'I hope so. With my claustrophobia I don't fancy growing old in a prison cell.'

Evans laughed and returned his attention to the road. It was all right for him. He was probably used to driving round in police vehicles, even if he wasn't usually behind the wheel.

Casually he swung the van toward the main gates, the forbidding walls towering above us. A face peered out through the grille, disappeared and, a few seconds later, the huge gates began to swing open. Committed now, we drove slowly into the courtyard and I was barely able to suppress a shudder as the gates clanged shut behind us. Apparently I was the only one to be affected, for, within seconds of switching off the ignition, Evans had produced a battered pack of Embassy and was delving in his pocket for a light. Reluctantly I slid open the door and dropped heavily to the ground. The rear door was already open and one of Evans's boys, looking surprisingly smart in his blue uniform, was clambering out. He too was completely unmoved, giving me a wink as I stood straightening my tunic.

The next part was entirely up to me and it was relatively straightforward. With a ramrod back I strode toward the reception area, breathing deeply of the frosty morning air. Inside it wasn't much warmer and I stood by the door for a moment, rubbing my hands together and looking at the prisoner, guarded by a couple of warders, who was sitting on the bench, a lean, nondescript man with his frizzy hair receding at the temples. A momentary flicker of his gray eyes showed he'd recognized me. He was probably wondering what the hell was going on because nobody had told him he was due to be rescued. I turned away and approached the counter.

'You're early, aren't you?' the warder said in a surly voice, glancing at the clock on the wall.

'It's our first time on the run,' I explained, and jerked a thumb at Sutters. 'Is that the one?'

'That's right,' the warder admitted vaguely, accepting the papers I'd offered him. 'Haven't I seen you somewhere before?'

It didn't say a lot for my disguise but the remark proved he had remarkable powers of observation. He'd only seen me once, nearly a year before, and he'd still recognized me although I'd gone to considerable pains to change my appearance. However, he wasn't sure enough of himself to probe any deeper and I certainly wasn't going to stop him from dropping the question. Hastily I signed the receipts for Sutters and followed the two warders as they shepherded their charge out into the courtyard. So far everything had gone exactly as Evans had predicted, and I was beginning to feel slightly more cheerful. Now there were only about a hundred things that could go wrong.

The prisoner was locked in the back of the van, I said a far from tearful farewell to the two warders, then I was back on the front seat beside Evans.

'Took your time, didn't you,' he said, grinning as he started the engine. 'I was beginning to think you must like it here.'

'Save the humor,' I told him. 'We're not out yet.'

Evans broadened his smile and eased us toward the gates. He had good nerves, I had to admit, but he had everything going for him. He'd probably spent so much time as a guest of the government already that he could do another ten years standing on his head. I couldn't, not unless I was imprisoned in Holloway. Only when we were outside on the road did I allow my confidence to slip up another notch, a mood which lasted all of a minute.

'The stupid sod,' Evans said disgustedly. 'Harry's fouled it up.'

Without looking I knew exactly what he meant. Harry had been running interference, supposedly delaying the official Black Maria. As I watched it approach from the opposite direction, sedately heading for the prison, it was painfully obvious that something had gone seriously wrong. When the two vehicles passed Evans raised his hand in comradely greeting, a gesture reciprocated by the other driver, then he really put his foot down. This time pedestrians did turn to look and neither of us gave a damn. In less than five minutes the prison officials would realize someone had abducted their prize charge from under their noses; five minutes after that, half the Metropolitan Police would be alerted and on the lookout for our van. Although we'd allowed thirteen minutes for the stage in the Black Maria, Evans drove like a maniac to manage it in eight, breaking every existing traffic law at least twice on the way.

If Harry had let us down, the boys waiting in the yard of the furniture depository were right on the ball. They began opening the gates as we entered the side street and Evans barely had to reduce speed as we slued left into the yard, the huge removal van perfectly positioned so that we had no need to alter course before mounting the ramp. Within less than a minute the doors were closed behind us and we were on our way again.

Up to this point we'd made it easy for the police, from there on they'd have to earn their money. We were in the truck for a little more than a quarter of an hour and it was time well spent. When we drove into the warehouse Evans had hired for the occasion, we were both in civilian clothes, as were Sutters and the two members of Evans's gang in the back. As soon as we'd stopped, I went round to let them out. Sutters was still bewildered but he had the sense not to ask any questions, preferring to wait until we were alone.

Once I was satisfied nothing had been left behind, all the fingerprints sprayed into oblivion, I jumped down from the removal van. Sutters was making like a corpse and his coffin was being shoved into the back of a hearse while Evans and the rest of his boys were piling into a Ford Escort. Evans, acting as decoy, was leaving the way we'd come; the hearse was slipping out through the back entrance. I went the same way as Evans. It was closer to the Tube.

Julie, the stray girl I'd taken in, was packed ready to leave when I arrived back at the flat.

'I'm just off, Philis,' she said breezily. 'I've tidied up the flat.'

Looking around the sparkling, alien living room I had to admit she was quite domesticated. It wouldn't take me more than a month to make it comfortable again.

'Thanks a lot,' I said nobly. 'Any idea where you're going?'

There was more than common civility behind my question. After the first night she hadn't used the spare bedroom, maintaining it was too cold, and I'd raised no objections when she'd moved into my bed. If it hadn't been for my work I would have been only too happy for her to continue as my guest.

'I'm going to stay with my uncle,' she told me. 'He's wired me some money.'

This was the first I'd heard of any uncle but her arrangements seemed reasonable enough. I wondered what else there was to say and apparently there was nothing. Julie stretched up, wrapped her arms round my neck and kissed me with considerable fervor.

'Good-bye,' she said in a voice to go with the kiss. That's just to remember me by.'

She picked up her suitcase and I opened the door for her, saving Henry Tate the need to ring. Julie blew me another kiss, then ran down the stairs, watched appreciatively by Tate.

'This is an unexpected pleasure, Henry,' I said jovially, being less than honest.

The visit was unexpected all right but it gave me about as much pleasure as a boot in the groin. Tate knew just how I was feeling and was well past the age when he bothered with polite trivialities, merely strolling past me into the living room. To build up the tension he lit his pipe, puffing away until it was drawing satisfactorily before he said anything. He'd probably been taking lessons from Pawson.

'Can you think of any good reason why I shouldn't have you arrested?' he asked from inside his personal smoke screen.

It was a highly pertinent question and I gave it serious consideration. Whichever way I looked at it the answer was the same.

'No,' I admitted, 'but you might remember we're on the same side.'

The answer pleased him enormously and I knew I'd said

the right thing. I only had to keep it up and he'd see I was let off with twenty years.

'Is Pawson likely to pull any strings if you are arrested?' he continued.

This was a less complicated question. Once the police had me I was on my own. Pawson had made this perfectly clear in his final briefing.

'Not a chance,' I said. 'He'll probably go into court and testify against me. He might do something once the fuss has blown over, but only if it doesn't threaten his relations with the police.'

'Good.' Tate beamed. 'Tell me all about it.'

'For God's sake, Henry,' I protested. 'You know I can't do that. Pawson would have my guts for garters.'

'Think of the alternative, Philis. Anyway, who's going to tell him? I'm not.'

'Surely you're not serious. You know there must be good reasons for all this. You're not going to shop me just because I refuse to tell you what they are.'

'I wouldn't bank on that,' Tate said softly. 'Sutters is a Soviet agent; you helped him to escape from prison. I want to know why.'

'Why not ask Pawson?'

'I'm asking you.'

Suddenly I realized Tate was deadly serious, and what he was asking me to do was against the first principles of my job, even if he was on the same side. My training had been comprehensive and one point had been hammered home time and time again: that the most heinous crime I could possibly commit was to divulge information, to any-one whomsoever. On the other hand I had a brain and couldn't see how my being incarcerated in an English jail

was going to benefit anyone, least of all me. Accordingly I
told Tate about our plans for Schnellinger, Klemper and
company.

The one thing I drew the line at was disclosing Sutters's
hiding place. Of course, in the interests of interdepart-
mental rivalry, Tate still tried to find this out, playing his
cards cleverly. When I left my flat I flushed the two tails I
was expected to, dropped them and was then supposed to
drive blithely to where Sutters was waiting. Knowing
Tate, I wasn't fooled for a moment, realizing that for the
next few days foreign agents could remove our secret instal-
lations stone by stone and he couldn't care less. Tate
wanted an edge over Pawson and he'd have every available
operative following me if this helped him to achieve his
aim.

The flying shuttle system he employed, involving four
different cars, took a lot of losing but I managed it, abandoning my own car in the process. In fact I was only a
quarter of an hour late when I arrived at the flat Sutters
was temporarily occupying, a mere stone's throw from the
American Embassy. Rob opened the door to me.

'Good evening, sir,' he said politely.

He didn't actually touch his forelock but he came close
to it. Since I'd massaged his tonsils with my gun he'd
showed marked signs of respect. It could even be that I
frightened him.

'O.K. Rob, you can clear off now,' I told him.

Sutters was sitting in an armchair reading a newspaper
when I went into the living room. I hadn't expected a
warm welcome and I didn't receive one, having to settle
for a hostile glare. From the way he was examining me it
seemed likely he was debating which limb to break first.

'Who's looking after Wolf?' he demanded, dispensing with the usual pleasantries.

'Don't worry about the dog,' I assured him. 'He's getting plenty of exercise. We'll arrange to ship him anywhere you like, along with the rest of your chattels.'

This appeared to mollify him slightly. Although he still wasn't overfriendly he'd abandoned the idea of physical violence.

'Exactly what would have happened if you hadn't been able to spring me?' he asked curiously.

'There was never much danger of that. Evans makes his living helping people to escape from prison.'

'That's no guarantee he has to succeed every time. He might have made a mistake.'

'In that case you'd have been sent down for about a hundred years and I'd have been in the cell next door,' I told him. 'Read this. It's from Petrov.'

I tossed him the envelope and amused myself with a copy of *Penthouse* while he digested the instructions. This didn't take him very long.

'Well, pardner,' he said when he'd finished, overdoing both the western accent and the sarcasm, 'it seems I'm stuck with you. Is it all right to use the phone?'

'Go ahead. It's safe this end.'

His conversation with Petrov was brief and in Russian, which meant I couldn't follow it too well. From the number of times the name Philis cropped up, I caught the general drift though and was pleased to see Petrov's answers satisfied Sutters. He actually smiled at me after he'd replaced the receiver, a great step forward.

'There must have been an easier way to arrange this,' he commented.

'There probably was,' I admitted, 'but not in the time at

our disposal. Having you behind bars while we negotiated seemed a good idea. Your superiors were hardly likely to cooperate unless we had something to bargain with.'

Sutters returned to his armchair and lit a cigarette.

'So we pool information.'

'Pool away,' I told him. 'I haven't anything to contribute. We raided Combes Manor and didn't find a thing, no records, no correspondence, not even anything in the wastepaper baskets. All we collected were a lot of dead bodies and your name.'

'Klemper knew you were coming.'

It was a statement.

'Yes, he was on to Tracey.'

The Russian tapped ash from his cigarette, looking pensive. He wasn't impressed by my contribution.

'Their security is good,' he said. 'I've spent three months without getting anywhere. I'm no nearer to discovering who Schnellinger is or where to find him.'

'You'd better have something,' I threatened. 'Otherwise I might as well hand you back to the police.'

'Try it,' Sutters threatened in turn, showing he hadn't enjoyed his short sojourn in jail. 'Anyway, I am one step ahead of you. I think I know how to find Klemper.'

A curriculum vitae of Heinrich Klemper wouldn't have made pleasant reading, what he'd done to Tracey paling into insignificance beside some of his other achievements. Mass murder had been common enough in German-occupied Poland during the war, and many of the men responsible had appeared at Nuremberg or later tribunals. Klemper, however, hadn't been among them as he'd never made the mistake of leaving any witnesses. Watreb had been an example. In 1939 it had been a prosperous Polish village, a local agricultural centre with some five hundred inhabitants. At the end of the war it was a ghost village, a collection of derelict buildings, population nil. The same had been true of Plevny, a village some seventy-five miles to the northwest. In both cases, not to mention several smaller incidents, there had been speculation concerning a young German officer called Klemper, but with so many bigger fish to fry he'd been passed over. Even the Israelis had had no interest in him.

After the war his life had been shrouded in mystery. He'd surfaced briefly in Argentina, a high-ranking member of Perón's security police with an unsavory reputation as a successful interrogator, and Pawson's predecessor had toyed with the idea of utilizing his known predilection for little boys. This was why his photograph featured in the SR(2) files. Then, for nearly twenty years, he had dropped out of sight, only to reappear four years before when Schnellinger had commenced operations. Schnellinger remained a name unclothed with flesh and blood, the reason for Klemper's sudden importance. He'd been seen in Madrid at the time of Roger Brookes's abduction, then again in England shortly afterward, and he was the man most likely to tell us where to find his present employer. Unfortunately, with Tracey's death we'd lost him. Apparently this was a gap in our knowledge that Sutters was able to fill.

'Tell me more,' I suggested.

Villa Rosa, Spain, January 1972

Roger Brookes sat on the patio overlooking the sea, watching José gather together the lunch things. He felt weak, enervated, not nearly strong enough for what had to be

done. It was a fortnight now since they'd stopped pump-
ing him full of the so-called truth drugs, Pentothal, sco-
polamine and the like, finally realizing this wasn't the way
to make him talk, but they still kept him under sedation,
depressants which sapped his energy and his will. None-
theless, Brookes had maintained some grip on himself,
sufficient to force him into the course of action he saw as
his only hope. Klemper was bound to return soon and
Brookes had no illusion about what this would entail.

José, limpid-eyed, olive-skinned, gigolo extraordinary,
departed for the kitchen with the last of the dishes, and
Brookes rose wearily to his feet. The movement attracted
the immediate attention of Hans, his guard of the moment,
a pasty-faced lout in complete contrast to the Spaniard.
Whereas José was a woman killer in the romantic sense
Hans was a killer, period.

'Where are you going?'

'Where do you think' Brookes answered, his voice list-
less.

'Again?'

Said with a laugh. The state of the prisoner's bowels
had become a standing joke.

The lavatory was on the first floor, no key or bolt on the
inside. Once the door was closed behind him Brookes
pulled the already bent dessert spoon from his pocket, bent
it some more with his foot, wrapped it in his handkerchief
and quietly jammed it under the door. Although it could
hardly be described as the perfect wedge, it did offer him
a certain degree of protection against interruption. With
any luck he had ten minutes, perhaps a quarter of an hour,
before it would be needed.

As a first step Brookes removed the wire screen covering

the small window, relatively simple to do since he'd been loosening it for some days, and leant it carefully against the wall. His shoes off, the window opened, he pulled himself up onto the sill, maneuvering himself into a sitting position. Already his exertions had left him drenched with sweat and there was no sign of the surge of adrenalin he'd been hoping for. Where he was, Brookes was in full view of anyone in the garden, neatly framed by the pale pink walls of the villa, but there was nobody to see him. José was still busy in the kitchen, Nestor was on duty at the gate and Hans was stationed on the landing outside the bathroom; otherwise Brookes wouldn't have been where he was. The only gamble was his own strength.

Gulping great mouthfuls of air into his lungs, steadying his breathing, Brookes examined the drainpipe some six feet to his left, selecting his handhold with care. The sound of a sudden cough from Hans, the cough of a three-packs-a-day man, did nothing to disturb his concentration. Satisfied that the distances were right, he used his trousers to wipe his hands free of perspiration, stood up on the windowsill, turning so that his face was to the wall, and stretched for the drainpipe. The fingers of his right hand found a grip on the warm metal, leaving him spread-eagled across the wall, one hand still clutching the frame of the window. Even as he prepared to transfer his full weight to the drainpipe Brookes knew his arms weren't strong enough. When Hans and José reached him, less than two minutes later, the Englishman lay sprawled on the flagstones of the patio, some twenty feet below the open bathroom window.

5

AFTER AN IMPRESSIVE BUILD-UP Sutters's information proved to be something of an anticlimax and, although he might have thought he could find Klemper, I wasn't nearly so sure. The sum total of the KGB's research, subject to the same difficulties which had hampered us, was hardly more impressive than our own. From 1945 until he came into prominence as Schnellinger's chief executive officer, Klemper's life had been a complete blank as far as the Russians were concerned, and there had been only one way to fill it in. Starting with a list which must have been half a mile long, containing the name of every person who could claim a nodding acquaintance with Klemper prior to the end of the war, they had worked through them one by one. After three years' hard work Moscow had a second list two miles long and the same photograph we had, taken in Argentina in 1949.

Amongst the apparently useless information they'd dug up was the fact that Klemper had been ambidextrous, had liked little girls as well as little boys. Under this heading they had dug up the name of his procuress, a Master-Kalefactress at one of the Polish female labor camps, a particularly repellent type by the name of Elsa Schacht. However, like every other avenue the Russians had explored, the end of hostilities had seemingly brought about a complete break in the relationship. Elsa had married an English corporal who had been unaware of her background, had set up house in Manchester and had been widowed three years later when her husband had used slightly too much gelignite on the safe he had been endeavoring to open. After a decent period of mourning Elsa had obtained a job in a local factory, allowed the occasional man into her bed to check everything was in working order and, in general, led a life of such boring normality it was a wonder she hadn't landed a part in "Coronation Street." This was all very disappointing for the KGB, although, long before they'd reached this point, they'd already decided they were on the wrong tack. Accordingly they were trying to penetrate Schnellinger's organization, along with the Americans, British and Swahilis, bumping head on into the same cutouts which had concussed everybody else.

Then, six months previously, someone in the CIA had had his brainstorm and bought Schnellinger lock, stock and barrel, securing his and Klemper's undivided services for the Americans. The response in Moscow had been similar to their probable reaction to an attempt to blow up Lenin's tomb. Suddenly the Russians' new interest in Klemper, as their only line to Schnellinger, made their previous attitude seem like idle curiosity. One of the first things they'd done had been to recheck their original findings and one very interesting fact had emerged. Widow O'Malley, née Schacht, had made good since they'd last screened her. From being a £12-a-week factory worker in Manchester she had become the proprietor of a chic boutique in Nottingham. This was quite a big step, with no apparent reason for her affluence, and it was at this stage that Sutters had been brought in. After his investigations he had no doubt that the boutique was a front for a safe house and that Klemper was once more in touch with his old procuress.

Considering the effort put in, Sutters had to be optimistic, but I wasn't. Although I was prepared to accept the safe house, I maintained Klemper was hardly likely to leave a forwarding address lying around. At this point the discussion became slightly acrimonious, Sutters pointing out that Klemper had actually stayed at the boutique, had been followed to Combes Manor and had been lost only as a result of British inefficiency. In fact he was even more specific, delivering a barbed harangue on the defects of SR(2).

The upshot was that Sutters spent two days in a farmhouse near Swaffham, just to let the police get used to the idea of having lost him. For my part, I went to Nottingham. All I learned was that I liked the Bridgeford Hotel, the people of Nottingham would vote for Enoch Powell in a landslide and Elsa Schacht wasn't doing very well with her boutique. When Sutters joined me I was eager to discover how efficient she was at running a safe house.

The boutique was situated in one of the more unfashionable parts of Nottingham, looking sadly out of place at the end of a long row of grimy, terraced houses, its only competitors two pubs, a tobacconist and a betting shop. It was made up of two houses knocked together and Elsa lived above the shop, an arrangement which suited us. Both Sutters and I were agreed on the direct approach, seeing no need for elaboration. The only people likely to interfere with our plans were two young female assistants, who left in a rush as soon as the shop closed for the day, and a rabbity little man, a kind of all-round dogbody. Combined with one middle-aged German woman he hardly constituted a threat and neither of us anticipated any trouble. My only slight reservation was whether Elsa could actually tell us anything worthwhile.

Closing time for the boutique was 5.30 P.M. and we arrived there about a minute before the doors were due to be locked. There were no other customers, hardly surprising considering our combined observations had told us Elsa was lucky if she made more than a dozen sales a day, and only one of the assistants was in evidence, a blatantly artificial blonde whose great ambition in life seemed to be to use a cake of mascara and a stick of lipstick every week. She came over immediately, obviously eager to be off.

'Were you looking for anything in particular?' she asked with all the refinement of a pronounced Nottingham accent.

'Actually,' I told her, 'we were hoping for a word with Mrs. O'Malley.' This was Elsa's married name. 'Could you tell her she has visitors.'

'Actually,' the girl mimicked unkindly, 'I could.'

The assistant headed toward the back of the shop, examining the business card which said my name was Jackson and that I worked for a fictitious wholesaler. I joined Sutters, who was browsing through the stock with a bemused expression on his face. Wordlessly he indicated a dress which had been designed along the lines of a fishing net and dyed a tasteful shade of purple. It was a real bargain at £12.

'Reactionary,' I said. 'Haven't you heard of free expression?'

Any prospect of a stimulating ideological discussion was ruined by the reappearance of the shop assistant. From the way she was rushing around it was obvious she wasn't paid overtime.

'Mrs. O'Malley will see you in the office,' she announced, already turning on her heel.

Obediently we followed her through into Elsa's office, a windowless room lined with dress racks and box-filled shelves. Personally, I would have called it a stock room with a desk and filing cabinet thrown in, but I had nothing against people who liked euphemisms. Elsa, somebody who presumably did like them, was sitting behind the desk. She was another peroxide blonde with a desire to help out the cosmetic manufacturers, only she had more excuse for her lavish use of make-up. Her jowls were developing bloodhound characteristics, the crow's-feet were growing into ostrichfeet and she had a weight problem which made the skimpy green minidress ridiculous and slightly obscene. A bell tent and a yashmak were more in order.

'All right, Greta,' Elsa said. She must have learned her English from an American without quite losing her German accent, then her years in England had added a layer or two of Mancunian overtones. It made for a fascinating combination. 'Lock up, then you and Helen can go.'

Greta didn't need to be told twice, probably envisaging an exciting evening at the Sherwood Rooms, and as soon as she was out of the room Elsa returned her attention to the books. It was a good five minutes before she again acknowledged our presence, flashing us a winning smile. It was the kind of smile you could see any night of the week at the Long Bar in Manchester.

'What can I do for you, gentlemen?' she asked, without telling us to take a seat.

This was because there weren't any spare chairs.

'I'm afraid the business card was a blind,' Sutters answered, coming straight to the point. 'We came here because we're trying to locate an old acquaintance of yours. A man called Heinrich Klemper.'

'Oh?'

Elsa raised her heavily penciled eyebrows, more out of politeness than surprise.

'You're not denying you know him?'

Sutters was the one who was surprised and he had me for company.

'Why should I?'

By now Elsa and Sutters had thrown so many unanswered questions at one another I thought it was time I took a hand. Elsa's attitude was completely wrong and it made me nervous, prompting me to suspect that we'd been far too casual in our approach.

'Can you tell us when you last saw Klemper?' I inquired, wondering what we'd overlooked.

'If you're really interested, Philis, it was about a fortnight ago,' Elsa told me, giving her first direct answer and displaying a disconcerting familiarity with my identity. 'You can come out now, Frank.'

Frank was the rabbity little man I'd seen when I'd had the boutique under observation and the gun he was holding showed he was the point we'd overlooked. I'd placed him as the general factotum, nothing more, some masculine muscle to hump the heavier loads. Sutters had reached the same conclusion, and he'd had Elsa under observation for three months, but this didn't excuse our mistake. We'd been overconfident, had neglected elementary precautions, and when Frank emerged from the racks of dresses on my left we were taken off guard.

'Put your hands on your heads,' Frank ordered, nervous despite the gun.

Although Sutters and I had never worked together before, we performed quite creditably after a startled exchange of glances, a silent admission of carelessness. Sutters moved a shuffling step to his right, attracting the attention of both Elsa and Frank, and I dived at Frank, knocking his gun aside and hitting him in the chest with my shoulder. Off balance, Frank went into the dress racks, striking the floor with his back, all the air driven from his lungs by my weight on top of him. We were both enshrouded in yards of material, but I had the wrist of Frank's gun hand in a grip that wasn't going to be broken and, inspired by the muffled crack of Sutters's gun in the room behind me, I hit Frank twice. With his gun held loosely in my left hand I extricated myself from the dresses, not bothering about the damage I did to the stock.

'Drop it,' Elsa said as I emerged. 'Then put your hands behind your neck.'

Without hesitation I did as I'd been told, sadly aware that I'd misinterpreted the significance of the silenced shot. Elsa was still comfortably seated at the desk, holding a Mauser the size of a small antitank gun, a cylindrical extension on the business end, while Sutters leant against the wall near the door, looking decidedly unhappy. From the way he was clutching his right shoulder it wasn't difficult to guess why.

'I'm sorry, Philis,' he said, his attempted smile spoiled by a grimace of pain. 'She had the cannon in her lap.'

My nod of acknowledgment was on the curt side, my attention focused on Elsa, waiting for her to pronounce sentence. It was another mistake. Once a vengeful Frank had retrieved his gun he wasted no time in pistol whipping me from behind.

As if the ache in my head wasn't bad enough I came round to find myself lying on a hard, stone floor with my arms tied behind my back. There was also someone doing his honest best to cave in my ribs with a foot or knee. Painfully I turned my head and opened my eyes, something of a waste of time as I couldn't see a thing. To show how much I was enjoying life I tried a groan or two.

'Philis, you bastard,' Sutters's voice said affectionately. 'Can you hear me?'

'I think so,' I muttered thickly, deciding my head wasn't too bad after all. 'Where are we?'

'In the cellar, where else. How do you feel?'

'A lot better since you stopped kicking me. You'd better brush up on your first aid. As I remember, it isn't one of the recommended techniques for reviving patients with concussion.'

'I'm glad you're feeling so cheerful,' Sutters told me, more than a trifle acidly. 'I always thought you'd die with a smile on your lips.'

My immediate reaction was to subject the knots holding me to a thorough examination, only to discover they were as secure as I'd anticipated. Houdini or any fully trained contortionist might have slipped out easily enough but I couldn't.

'You're sure?' I asked. 'About dying, I mean.'

'Positive.' Sutters's tone certainly carried conviction. 'Apparently Frank has a nice quarry in the country lined up for you.'

'In that case we'd better do something.'

'You'd better do something,' Sutters retorted. 'My right arm is completely useless and they're not going to kill me anyway. They want me alive.'

Callous wasn't the word for Sutters's attitude, but I thought I'd better rescue us just the same. I never had wanted to be buried in a quarry.

My first idea didn't work. I couldn't free myself, I couldn't untie the ropes binding Sutters's wrists and he couldn't release me, which left us both tied up in the cellar with the threat of execution over my head. Obviously some sharp-edged implement was called for, like a knife or a piece of broken glass, and this led me to embark on a tour of inspection. Once again it was wasted effort, the cellar bare, just walls, floor, ceiling and us. Disconsolately I stumbled back to where Sutters was propped against the wall.

'No go?' he inquired.

'Not a thing.'

By this time I was no longer feeling at all cheerful, my only slight consolation the conviction that whatever else fate had in store I wasn't destined to die at the hands of a comic opera couple like Elsa and Frank. Fair enough, we'd made a bad mistake, but our captors weren't too clever either, otherwise they wouldn't have been in charge of a safe house. They'd already made one mistake themselves, not killing me while I was unconscious, and there had to be some way I could take advantage of this.

Unfortunately I still couldn't see how to get rid of the ropes round my wrists. If Elsa had left me my cigarette lighter there would have been no problem, but she hadn't. All my pockets were empty, this had been the first thing I'd checked. Or had I?

'John,' I said, 'we may be in business. There used to be a nail file in the outside breast pocket of my jacket.'

It was still there although, with our hands tied behind our backs, discovering this was no easy process. Even when Sutters had succeeded in teasing the file from my top pocket, our problems were a long way from being over. Ordinary rope was made from several strands of cord, each strand containing a large number of yarns. The yarns were twisted together, increasing tenacity, then the strands were also twisted around each other in the opposite direction to the twist of the yarns. Any idiot knew this, the same way he knew about the resultant tensile strength. What the average layman wasn't likely to realize was how difficult it was to saw through a piece of nonrotten rope with an ordinary nail file, especially when the rope was binding your wrists together behind your back.

Sutters was no help at all, unable to do the job for me. With the file clamped in numbed fingers I rubbed it backward and forward across the rope with no sign of success to spur me on. For all I knew the rope could be nylon reinforced, which meant I was wasting my time. I was still sawing away when Elsa and Frank came for me.

The sudden illumination was dazzling after the hours in the dark, a complete surprise because the light switch was outside the cellar. Blinking owlishly, I barely had time to conceal the file before the door opened and our hosts descended the three steps. Elsa emphasized her leadership by standing a pace in front of Frank, scrutinizing us both intently.

'How's the shoulder?' she asked, addressing Sutters.

He didn't bother to answer. Now the light was on I

could see his bloodstained shirt had been ripped open and his wound neatly bandaged. Even so, he was looking positively haggard, a good five years older than when I'd last seen him. Shock plus loss of blood was my instant diagnosis.

'I could do with an aspirin,' I volunteered. 'My head hurts.'

Elsa ignored my remark as comprehensively as Sutters had ignored her question.

'Get Philis on his feet,' she instructed Frank.

In the process Frank managed to hurt my head some more, lifting me by my hair.

'Say good-by to your friend,' he sneered once he had me on my feet. 'You won't be meeting again.'

There was to be no hero's farewell. Sutters didn't say a word, just winked as the other two turned away. He'd been watching the rope when I'd tried to pull my wrists apart.

Elsa relocked the cellar door while Frank amused himself by prodding me in the kidneys with his gun, then we set off in convoy. Our immediate destination was the back yard, where a Bedford van was waiting, and I felt increasingly confident with every step. Nobody was going to shoot me on the premises and Sutters's wink had confirmed my suspicion that there was a lot more play in the ropes around my wrists. I didn't even mind going for a ride, part of the way anyway.

'In the van,' Frank ordered.

Awkwardly I did as he suggested, settling down on the metal floor, eager for them to close the doors so I could resume work with the nail file. First Frank tied my ankles, what I hoped was a wasted precaution. Satisfied my legs were secure, Frank was about to clamber out of the van when Elsa stopped him.

'Check his wrists as well,' she said.

This was when I realized she could never be a bosom friend. Resignedly I allowed Frank to roll me on my face. Obviously he had a lot of pride in his knot-tying ability because he was content with a perfunctory tug.

'He won't get away,' he announced.

'Do the job properly,' Elsa came back, effectively putting a damper on my hopes. 'You can't possibly see in this light.'

Muttering something about bloody women under his breath, an attitude I heartily endorsed, Frank provided some illumination with the cigarette lighter he'd taken from me. That was when he noticed the nail file I was clutching tightly in my sweating palm.

As we cruised down Carlton Road there were only the two of us in the Bedford, Frank and myself, proving Elsa wasn't anywhere near as efficient as she seemed to think. With only Frank to bother about I hoped the nail file was super-fluous.

Unaware of my thoughts, Frank drove into the city center before bearing left toward Trent Bridge, passing little other traffic as it was after midnight. Patiently I waited until we were on the Grantham Road, the city of Nottingham well behind us.

'Pull into the side of the road,' I shouted above the noise of the engine, satisfied we'd traveled far enough. 'I want to talk to you.'

'What is there to talk about?' Frank shouted back, not turning his head.

'If you switch off the engine I can tell you without losing the skin from the back of my throat,' I answered, my voice still at a low bellow.

Frank drove a few hundred yards, thinking my suggestion over, then pulled into the side of the road. It was an opportunity for me to slide a foot closer to the back of the driver's seat.

'What is it?' Frank asked, swiveling his head.

'I would have thought that was obvious,' I told him. 'I don't want to die. How much does it cost for you to let me go?'

Frank shook his head derisively, very sure of himself.

'There isn't enough money,' he said. 'I want to live as well.'

'Fair enough,' I agreed. 'You're scared of Klemper, and I can't blame you, but kill me and you're a dead man. Let me go and I'll guarantee you're protected.'

It wasn't a very convincing speech and wasn't meant to be, I was merely offering him a chance he didn't deserve. For answer Frank laughed and tugged at the starter, leaving me free to concentrate on my next move.

This was the kind of thing anyone with a reasonably supple body could do, providing he realized he was going to be shot if it didn't come off. The van covered a good ten miles while I satisfied myself everything was right, then I performed my version of the coiled spring. Starting with my head down between my knees, I threw my torso back, levered up with my shoulder and arms, twisted to align myself and clubbed the back of Frank's neck with my feet. The speedometer must have been registering forty at the time, a fair rate of progress considering the wintry conditions, and the heels of my shoes did nothing for Frank as a driver. With his head driven forward against the windshield, he struggled desperately to retain control before the van plowed into the snow-covered bank at the side of the road, the crash banging my face painfully against the seat.

Using the seat for support I forced myself to my feet, ignoring the blood gushing from my nose, understandably anxious about countermeasures from the driver. My eyes were watering too much for me to see what he was doing so I had to operate by guesswork, jackknifing over the back of the bench seat on the passenger side, rolling onto my back and then driving my bound feet toward the spot I expected Frank's chin to be. If it had been there I might have been lucky and broken his neck cleanly, but it wasn't because Frank was already dead, sprawled over the wheel with his head through the shattered windshield. It wasn't a pretty sight and he would have been far wiser to have accepted my proffered bribe. That way he would have died a lot less messily.

Twenty minutes later I was free, a nasty burn on the inside of my left wrist to show where I hadn't been able to hold the cigarette lighter steady, but I didn't do anything else constructive for another ten minutes, preferring to moan quietly to myself as the circulation returned to my hands. In fact I could have managed longer if the ten minutes hadn't already been an overindulgence. I was still in the van when company arrived, a Panda-type car, blue light flashing merrily on the roof. Despite my great admiration for the police I wished the young constable hadn't come, not when I had a murdered man beside me.

'Are you all right, sir?' the policeman asked, a touch of unsuspecting concern in his voice.

'Not too bad,' I said weakly. By this time I was leaning against the side of the van, the policeman beside me. 'I think my friend is dead, though.'

Naturally enough the constable turned to take a look at Frank, the moment I chose to administer the carotid treatment. One of the great things about working for SR(2) was that I made friends everywhere.

London, England, January 1972

It had been an excellent meal, more than sufficient to fill Pawson with benevolence as he smoked his cigar, a kindly eye on the brandy in front of him. Replete, he was prepared to play along with his companion, an American. Naturally he would have preferred to be with a friend, but he had dined so well that the coming business was something he was prepared to endure.

'Well, Charles,' the American said expansively, coming in on cue, content in the knowledge that he'd offered his guest the best. 'How's business?'

'Couldn't be better,' Pawson answered serenely.

Beaumont laughed heartily, although Pawson hadn't been aware of saying anything amusing. Even the indulgent patronage implicit in the laugh failed to irritate him. Pawson was in a mood to admit that the CIA, with its plethora of money and men, made SR(2) seem very small beer in comparison. In the same way, he was prepared to admit that he'd never been responsible for a monumental balls-up like the Bay of Pigs.

'That's fine, Charles,' Beaumont went on. 'You're probably wondering why I invited you here so I'd better tell you.' This time his laugh suggested he thought he'd come up with something witty himself. Pawson smiled politely but said nothing. 'I've a proposition that should appeal to you.'

'You have?'

Although Pawson gave the impression of bestowing his undivided attention on Beaumont, he was keeping an appreciative eye on a blonde at the next table, admiring the generous plunge of her neckline. She was far too young, of course, but it all helped to keep the blood circulating.

'You bet I have,' Beaumont was saying. 'You're a pro, Charles, and you run a tight little outfit.' Another helping of condescension, Pawson noted automatically. 'I'd like to see more cooperation between our two departments.'

'Don't we cooperate already?' Pawson asked innocently.

'Of course we do, but on far too small a scale. There's too much duplication, rivalry if you like. Too many occasions when we risk fouling up an operation because we're at cross-purposes.'

'This is bound to happen,' Pawson pointed out, 'however deplorable we both agree it is. I don't see how it can be avoided.'

'There is an answer, though.' Beaumont emphasized his positive thinking with an aggressive, no-nonsense stab of his cigar, depositing a cylinder of ash on the crisp whiteness of the cloth. 'What we need is better demarcation, clarification of our spheres of interest.'

'I suspect you've oversimplified,' Pawson objected, speaking without heat.

'Perhaps I have, but the principle is valid. There are matters which are the exclusive concern of the United States and the same is true for British interests. At the moment the boundaries are far too blurred.'

'I see your point,' Pawson admitted. 'Surely it's something to be discussed at ministerial level.'

By now Pawson was thoroughly enjoying the postprandial blandishments, finding them unexpectedly entertaining. He knew perfectly well that this wasn't something to be discussed at a ministry. Behind the smile, the honeyed words and the cigar smoke the American was telling him to keep his hands off Schnellinger.

'There's too much red tape once a minister is brought in. I prefer to deal with somebody like you, Charles, somebody who's directly involved. You're in a position to appreciate the dangers. Unless some form of agreement is reached there could be real trouble.'

'You're so right,' Pawson agreed urbanely. 'Schnellinger is a perfect example.'

'Schnellinger?' Beaumont repeated uncertainly, wondering whether he'd been talking over Pawson's head.

'That's right. I'd hate to discover he's been working under American orders. He's just had one of my men tortured to death, in this country as well.'

Beaumont had no immediate answer and Pawson had no intention of waiting for him to think of one. It was as good an exit line as he was likely to come up with, unless he wanted to spoil a delightful evening.

6

My one-man crime wave was a long way from being over. With extreme reluctance I borrowed the Panda car, my official entry for the race to Elsa's boutique, the competitors being the police and myself, and the contest was the result of Elsa's crass inefficiency. Anyone who sent somebody off to be killed in a van with the inspiring motif 'O'Malley's Boutique' plastered on the sides in letters a yard high deserved to attract the attention of the police, but I didn't. The wisest thing for me to have done would have been to leave Nottingham far behind, a move which would have suited my own personal inclinations. Unfortunately I had to rescue John, although this was no case of noblesse oblige. If the police found him in Elsa's cellar he, great friend of mine that he was, would have no hesitation in broadcasting my name far and wide.

For the time being I wasn't much happier at the knowledge police control was busily transmitting information about the car I was driving. The repeated commands for me to come in over the radio had lasted a mere ten minutes. Since then there have been an ominous silence, a sure indication that it would be extremely unwise for me to drive right into the city. Sticking resolutely to the back roads, I dumped the car once I was in striking distance of the ring road, resigned to a long, cold walk to the nearest phone booth where I intended to send for a taxi. All the odds seemed to be in favor of a photo finish outside the shop.

It proved to be a dead heat. I had the taxi drop me a street away from my destination, covering less than a hundred yards on foot before the first police car passed me. As soon as it was out of sight I began to run, heading for the back entrance and hoping I reached it before the police thought to post a man there. After all, I'd learnt on my mother's knee that hitting people in blue uniforms was wrong.

The last stretch I took very cautiously and it was a relief to find the back yard deserted. There'd been a bunch of keys in Frank's pocket which I'd thought to bring with me, the second key fitting the lock to the back door. Inside, the building was quiet and dark, a residence with the occupants abed. Either that or Elsa had flown the coop. The silence also told me the police must be going the whole hog, intending a full-scale raid. For the moment they were still making their dispositions.

Using my hands to guide me I made for the cellar, reaching the door just as a loud knocking commenced at the front of the building. Elsa, bless her heart, had left the key of the cellar door in the lock and I didn't stay to listen to the hubbub. Sutters was lying on the floor, more or less where I'd left him, still pale but looking considerably healthier.

'My hero,' he said with breathless admiration. 'What took you so long?'

'Quiet,' I hissed. 'I brought the police with me.'

The news upset him and he muttered darkly under his breath while I untied his wrists, muttering a lot more when the blood started to return to his hands. Callously indifferent to his suffering I went back to the door, far more interested in what happening in the rest of the building. From the sound of voices in the shop I gathered not only that Elsa had been stupid enough to admit the police but that it was high time I left.

'Come on,' I whispered, impatient to be on my way.

'You have a plan?'

Sutters remained where he was, rubbing his forearms.

'Yes,' I exaggerated. 'We make a run for the back door. If there are police outside we'll have to persuade them to move out of our way. Nothing too rough, though.'

Sutters grinned, looking better every minute. He wasn't any more impressed with my suggestion than I was myself.

'Terrific. The product of a mastermind,' he sneered. 'It's the subtle blend of maximum violence and minimum finesse that really grabs me.' He paused, evidently thinking we had all the time in the world. 'Aren't you forgetting the whole reason for coming here? Without Elsa we've no lead to Klemper or Schnellinger.'

"Balls to Klemper and Schnellinger,' I retorted gracelessly. 'We won't find them in Nottingham jail and that's where we'll be unless we leave soon.'

'All right,' Sutters agreed. 'We leave but we're not doing it your way. Apart from being singularly unintelligent it's probably impossible.'

Sutters's quibbling was not only wasting valuable time but irritating me as well. Now the police were past the front door they'd be all over the building in a few minutes.

'I don't fancy the idea either,' I admitted, 'but I don't see an alternative. If you've anything better in mind spit it out and forget the sarcasm.'

Impatiently Sutters ran a hand through his frizzy hair.

As he was only two or three years away from baldness it didn't take him long.

'Of course I've a better idea,' he told me nastily. 'For a start you can lock the door.'

His suggestion immediately made me forgive him all his snide remarks and administer a few mental kicks to myself. Obediently I retrieved the key from the outside of the door, locked up and, as an afterthought, pocketed the key.

'So it's a safe house,' I said, still annoyed with myself. 'How can you be sure the bolt hole is down here? I can't see anything.'

'Looking at the walls is about all I've had to do for the last few hours,' Sutters replied. 'The exit is over here.'

He crossed to the far corner of the cellar, a section partly shrouded in shadow, and tapped the wall. Remaining by the door, I carefully inspected the spot he'd indicated. It still looked like any other piece of wall, the same uniform, grayish color as the rest of the cellar, not the slightest semblance of a crack to mark the hypothetical exit. Obviously John's eyesight was a lot better than mine because at closer quarters the result of my scrutiny was the same. Resorting to tactile investigation, I tried kicking it and, apart from the pain in my foot, this did nothing for me. With no hollow echo to reward me it was just like breaking a couple of toes on a brick wall anywhere in the world.

'Try using your hand,' Sutters suggested.

When I did I realized he was correct. The wall might look like brick but it felt like metal.

'It's an escape hatch all right,' I said admiringly. 'I'm surprised you noticed it.'

'It's a standard Russian design,' Sutters told me, treating me to a pitying look. 'The opening mechanism is in the door handle. You have to twist it in an anticlockwise direction.'

Back at the door I did as he'd said. Absolutely nothing happened.

'Now that was really something,' I commented. 'In future I'll call you Ali Baba.'

'The theory behind the photoelectric cell was first appreciated at the end of the nineteenth century,' Sutters began. 'Since then —'

He didn't have to continue because I already had the message. As I stepped away from the door, allowing the circuit to be completed, I realized there was a lot to be said for the technological revolution.

Eighteen hours later I was back in the street outside the boutique, the hours in between hectic ones. Sutters and I had headed straight for the hotel, pausing only to clean ourselves up. Even after this Sutters had looked far too much like a man who'd been shot, and he waited in the car while I went inside to settle the bill and collect our baggage. Although our abrupt departure in the small hours undoubtedly aroused the curiosity of the night porter, this was much better than being in residence if the police chose to make a spot check.

From Nottingham we followed the A52 to Derby, ditched the car in a car park and caught the first bus to Loughborough. It was most unlikely that the police would know whom they were looking for— Elsa certainly couldn't afford to tell them — but, if they should get lucky, the precautions were sufficient to keep them off our backs for a day or two.

When we were safely installed in our new lodgings, Sutters had an opportunity to put his feet up for a few hours, something I envied him as I hit the cold streets again. The chief reason we had come to Loughborough, quite apart from the need to find accommodation a comfortable distance from Nottingham, was Dr. Ferguson. With his shifty eyes, drink-veined nose and rumpled suit he wasn't a credit to the medical profession's image, bearing more resemblance to a back-street abortionist than a respectable G.P. In fact, this was exactly what he had been until his license to practice medicine had been revoked five years before. On the other hand, he was the only doctor I knew of in the area who would treat a bullet wound without asking awkward questions. Elsa might have thought Sutters's injury was nothing to worry about but I preferred even Ferguson's dubious medical judgment to hers. After three quarters of an hour's verbal sparring I'd convinced Ferguson I wasn't a police spy, arranged an appointment for Sutters during the afternoon and handed over an exorbitant sum of money. By the time I'd bought a second-hand car it was thirty-six hours since I'd last slept, my head was aching abominably and I had no difficulty in sleeping soundly for eight hours. It would have been longer but a freshly bandaged Sutters was ready to return to Nottingham.

On this occasion we went into the city with no intention of risking all our eggs in the same basket. Although Sutters and I hadn't really discussed the matter, there was a tacit admission that we'd been unforgivably careless the previous evening, the results almost disastrous. As usual Sutters had the easy job. All he had to do was rest his shoulder until the magistrate's court opened in the morning. Elsa was due to appear there at eleven and when she did we might want to pick her up. While she was assisting the police with their inquiries I intended to search her living quarters on the outside chance of finding some lead to Klemper. It was a long shot but if I did find something we wouldn't have to squeeze the information out of Elsa.

Essentially an optimist, I'd half expected to discover a policeman in the vicinity of the boutique, but after half an hour's stealthy prowling I hadn't found one. Both front and back the building was in pitch blackness, no light or flash of movement visible at any of the windows. Even so I didn't intend to find anyone lying in wait for me inside. Another hour of cold and cheerless observation went by and I was as certain as I was ever going to be that there was nobody there, time to move in.

As Frank's bunch of keys was still in my possession, I used the back door, and, once inside, I remained absolutely motionless for several minutes, ears straining to catch the slightest sound of movement. Again there was nothing and I permitted myself the luxury of relaxing. Earlier in the day I'd decided to restrict my search to the living room and Elsa's bedroom, not having enough time to cover the entire premises, and I took the living room first. An hour later I'd torn it to pieces, most of the time spent in opening the safe, unoriginally concealed behind a hideous painting of a pot of geraniums, and it was a complete waste of effort. The contents consisted of about two hundred pounds in cash, some cheap jewelery and a bunch of legal documents, none of which helped me. All Elsa's personal papers, letters and suchlike were inside an old-fashioned, roll-top desk and there was nothing in them to tell me where Klemper was. I hadn't expected much but if Elsa had been in contact with him it was reasonable to expect some clue to his whereabouts. Now it looked as thought Sutters and I had been building castles in the air.

There was still the bedroom but I didn't have any great

hopes. I went through the room with a fine-toothed comb — wardrobes, drawers, suitcases, the lot — and the result was a resounding blank. Every possible hiding place exhausted, I plumped down on the edge of the double bed, idly playing my pocket light around the room. This only served to show me I hadn't missed anything. For want of something better to do I picked up the paperback lying on the bedside table, amused to see it was a German edition of Ka-Tzetnik's *House of Dolls*. Probably it was a sign of nostalgia on Elsa's part, a longing for the good old days when she'd had a Konzentration Zenter of her own and had had no need to live vicariously. As I didn't read German I was about to replace the book when a piece of paper fell from between the pages, fluttering slowly to the floor. It was the flap of an envelope Elsa had been using as a bookmark and there was nothing to show it was of any interest. Apart from the West Berlin postmark, that is. The letter and the rest of the envelope could have been from anyone, from one of Elsa's relatives say, but I tucked the piece of paper in my wallet just the same. Suddenly I'd remembered something I'd found in the desk in the living room, something which had had no significance before.

Filled with a new sense of purpose, I returned to the living room, moving silently on the balls of my feet, more out of habit than anything else. It was lucky I did. I'd no sooner closed the living room door behind me than a sound from the rear of the building froze me in my tracks. Seconds later I heard the noise again and I doused my flashlight. My ears as sensitive as a bat's, I transferred it to my left hand and unholstered my gun. Somebody was forcing the lock on the back door and until I knew who it was I didn't intend to move an inch. The only thing I was certain of was that the intruder wasn't a policeman — the police would have had no need to break in.

A quarter of an hour later two other things had become apparent. The interloper was no burglar and he had no idea there was anybody else in the house. Whoever it was, he was doing the same job as me only he lacked my discrimination, going through every room he came to. Even so, he was moving fast. He'd already reached the kitchen, making the living room next on his itinerary, and when he came through the door he was due for quite a surprise.

Relaxed against the wall, I listened to the soft footsteps leaving the kitchen, coming toward me along the corridor. As the door swung open I flattened myself against the wall, inwardly amused by the confident way he came in, the hooded flashlight held nonchalantly in his right hand. Luckily for him I'd thought to draw the thick curtains. He'd taken a couple of steps into the room when I clipped him behind the ear with my gun, catching him under the armpits as he crumpled at the knees. It was only a gentle tap — I wanted to talk to him — but he'd be out for at least five minutes. To fill in time I switched on my flashlight and turned the unconscious man over with my foot. As I took in the smarmed-down hair, the weakly handsome face with its too fleshy lips, I was filled with a growing sense of wonder and incredulity.

In fact I was still standing like a dummy, trying to credit the evidence of my own eyes, when I sensed rather than heard a slight movement on the carpet behind me. Instinctively I ducked and twisted but I didn't have a chance, my sole achievement being to stop the cosh with my temple instead of the back of my head. There was no sensation of pain. Just a flashing white light, breaking up into a fuzzy red before I pitched gently forward into the traditional bottomless, black pit. That's what must have happened although I didn't know anything about it.

'You were coshed by a Chinaman,' somebody was saying. 'A tall Chinaman with a cast in his left eye.'

With my mouth pressed into the pile of the carpet I listened to the voice, wondering how one normal-sized head could be the source of so much pain. The headache didn't tempt me to argue with Sherlock Holmes. After all, in the fraction of a second before the cosh had landed, my flash had caught my assailant's face. He'd been a Chinaman all right, and he'd had a cast in his left eye. His face was embedded in my memory for all time, labeled as belonging to a man liable to assault me with blunt instruments.

'Joyce was with the Chinaman,' Sherlock droned on. 'That idiot Joyce isn't as big an idiot as everyone thinks. He's doubling for the Chinese.'

Again there didn't seem to be much point in argument. If pressed I could have suggested it wasn't beyond the realms of possibility for DI5 to have one or two Chinese in its employ. In that case, though, it was hardly likely one of them would be wasted on a routine search of a Nottingham boutique. Reluctantly I accepted the proposition that Joyce was working for the Chinese and waited for Sherlock to spout more words of wisdom. There was no great urgency about moving my face from the carpet. It seemed inconceivable that my head could hurt any more but I knew better. I'd been coshed before.

'Why didn't Joyce kill you?' the voice asked. 'If he's working for the Chinese he can't afford to leave you alive.'

With the posing of the $64,000 question I realized where

I'd heard the voice before. It was mine, albeit a trifle weak and indistinct, working overtime until I was fully conscious and in a fit state to restrict communication with myself to the confines of my cranium. This flash of insight led me to go through the argument again, arriving at the same conclusion. Joyce was doubling for the Chinese. Ergo, he had to kill me to protect himself. Q.E.D. The solitary flaw in my eminently logical deductions was that I was still alive. Battered, yes, but indisputably alive. Of course, Joyce might still be around, intending to finish me off at any moment. The thought made me involuntarily tense my muscles, the slight movement sending pain coursing from my head all the way to my coccyx. Almost immediately I relaxed, the pain ebbing slowly up my spine. There couldn't be anybody else on the premises. My ears had been alert from the instant consciousness had returned and all they'd picked up had been my own labored breathing and the occasional passer-by or motor car. The solution had to lie elsewhere.

Perversely I was unable to subdue a sneaking admiration for Joyce. There couldn't be many harder things for an intelligent man to do than to masquerade as a raving, imbecilic incompetent, a role he'd played to perfection. He'd even allowed me to take him apart without stepping out of character.

This train of thought brought back memories of his classic bomb in Pembrokeshire and of a sudden I was up on my feet, all but ignoring the blinding pain in my head. I didn't consider using the door for a moment. Instead I took three steps across Elsa's living room and jumped feet first through the front window, banking on the heavy curtains to stop me being cut to ribbons and luck to prevent both legs being broken by the fall. For a second I was lying on the ground, tangled up in the material, then I was pounding down the street, running for my life, each step driving a red hot nail into my skull.

The explosion came while I was still within fifty yards of the boutique, the blast picking me up like a rag doll. For almost a minute I hugged the cold pavement, waiting for the pieces of brick and mortar to stop pattering on my back, then I used a handy lamppost to pull myself to my feet. Looking back at the place where Elsa had once conducted her business, I had to admit it was a beautiful job, even though the explosion must have removed every window in the street. The neighbors on either side would have to evacuate while their houses were shored up and probably had painful bruises where they'd been bounced off the bedroom walls. Others would have had quite a bump when they were blown out of bed and a few people would have been cut by flying glass but, all things considered, it had been superbly done. Nobody was going to search Elsa's place and find anything Joyce had overlooked because the shop had been removed as neatly as a dentist would extract a tooth. It was almost as good a job as the one near Pembroke although until a few minutes before I'd believed, along with everyone else who'd heard of the incident, that Joyce must have had God up his rectum to have come out of it alive. Not everybody could blow up one of the explosives testing sheds around his ears and walk away without a mark on his body.

Sutters lounged lazily in his chair, the color returned to his cheeks. Typically, he'd made no offer to help me as I lay naked on the bed, picking slivers of glass out of my carcass with a pair of tweezers. A piece of plaster covered a gash on one palm, otherwise the curtains had protected me fairly well. Apart from my head, that is. Being hit by a blackjack in the hands of an expert was no joke, not even the morning after, and half a bottle of aspirin had done nothing to remove the nagging ache behind my eyes. The early-morning drive from Nottingham had done nothing to improve it either. We'd left Elsa alive and well and she'd undoubtedly be contacting Klemper once she was out of police custody, but this was no longer important.

'Joyce can't be all that clever,' Sutters remarked. 'He made a real mess of killing you. If I'd been in his place you wouldn't be here now. You'd be splattered all over Nottingham.'

I held back my reply until I'd eased out a particularly tricky fragment of glass from my shin. This was where most of the glass was, in the lower half of my legs, the disadvantage of going through a window feet first. All the same, if you knew the technique, it was a hell of a sight better than leading with your head. This might appear very spectacular at the cinema or on television, but when it was for real you risked everything from concussion to a slashed jugular. The glass came out and I dabbed Dettol on the cut.

'Fair enough, there was a mistake but it was more the Chinaman's fault than Joyce's,' I said. 'I could tap somebody on the head and tell you to within five minutes when he was likely to come round. If I said a man would be unconscious for an hour you'd believe me without question, the same as Joyce must have accepted what he was told. Joyce wasn't to know I turned my head before I was hit. The Chinaman should have done, even if my flashlight was in his face.'

The case for the defense concluded, I turned my attention to my left calf and Sutters lit a cigarette. He blew a couple of smoke rings to show how clever he was and I pulled out a couple of hairs, prompting a brief burst of profanity which didn't help my head.

'Judging by your language, your head must be better,' Sutters said. 'Perhaps you feel like answering a few questions.'

'Fire away,' I said generously, absorbed with my left leg. 'What do you want to know?'

'Just little things. Like why we've lost interest in Elsa. And whether you discovered where Klemper is.'

Most of the glass had been removed by now and I ditched the tweezers on the bedside table, beside the Dettol bottle.

'I would have thought it's obvious why we've lost interest in Elsa — it's too dangerous. Considering she's been connected with a murder, a bombing and bodily assault on a policeman in the last forty-eight hours, it's a fair bet the police are a wee bit suspicious.'

Sutters sighed disparagingly and rubbed his hand through his hair. It was an irritating habit, more than sufficient to justify his incipient baldness.

'You still haven't answered my question,' he persevered. 'If she's our only link to Klemper and Schnellinger we have to accept the risks, whatever they are.'

It was a really stirring speech, packed with heroism and a sense of duty. If he meant them, the sentiments made Sutters an out-and-out idiot.

'That's the spirit,' I said enthusiastically, risking a slipped disk as I bent to retrieve my underpants from the floor. 'Go back to Nottingham, John, and you can bank on my unqualified, hundred per cent support. I'll be in West Berlin.'

Washington, D.C., January 1972

'So what do we do?'

The unanswered question lay heavily in the air, none of the three other men at the oval table being tempted to interrupt. They all knew the speaker, a big, powerful man in every sense, and they could interpret his tone.

'Well, I'll tell you what we do,' Cowling continued, satisfied nobody was brash enough to interfere. 'We do nothing.'

Taggart and Carter absorbed the information without batting an eyelid, comfortably aware that they weren't directly involved, but Beaumont stirred uneasily in his chair. He was a patriot, a dangerous element in any intelligence agency.

'You mean just leave them to it,' he muttered, his face flushed.

'That's what I said,' Cowling answered icily.

For him the discussion was closed.

'But those bastards in London are waving two fingers at us,' Beaumont protested, a faint film of perspiration on his forehead.

'Let them,' Cowling told him, a nerve twitching in his right cheek, the first indication his temper was on the boil. 'We're not Schnellinger's nursemaid. We pay him for information.'

'How about the verbal pressure?' Taggart asked, deciding to go to Beaumont's aid. 'That doesn't cost us anything.'

Fingers drumming on the table, Cowling considered the suggestion.

'O.K.' he decided, 'but keep it low key. We'll leave it to Tom.'

Carter nodded absent-mindedly, only half aware of what had been said. His mind dwelt on the redhead who'd moved into the apartment across the hall, his mouth dry as he remembered it was his wife's night for the PTA.

7

WEST BERLIN was Europe's answer to Hong Kong, a glittering, capitalist showpiece jammed up the Communists' rump, and it was a city I'd always liked, mainly because I'd never been there. In fact, offhand, I couldn't think of a better place for a man in my profession not to be. This had nothing to do with the Germans living there. Rather, my attitude derived from the knowledge that the city was the world's stock market for traded information, with more agents to the square yard than any other area I could think of. Definitely not the city for a top-echelon intelligence operative to find himself, or even somebody like me.

During the long trek through the passenger hall at Tempelhof I amused myself by trying to spot the people taking my photo, not with standard Brownies but with sophisticated, miniaturized gadgets concealed in everything from toupees to fly buttons. Even allowing for a stop to watch the dogs piddling on the statue commemorating the Air Lift, I only managed to identify two camera fiends before I boarded a taxi, meaning I'd probably missed double that number. Not that an accurate head count bothered me, only the man who'd be taking news of my arrival back to Schnellinger's representative. Every intelligence agency in town would hear of it within twenty-four hours, but one man should be expecting me and he'd probably hear the glad tidings well before the rest of the field.

With this to cheer me on my way I sank back in my seat and allowed the taxi driver to maneuver his vehicle through the snarl of traffic, en route to my hotel in the neon jungle off the Kurfurstendamm.

My first three hours in West Berlin weren't exactly packed with industry, spent full length on my hotel bed while I wondered what kind of furor my appearance would have provoked. Coming into the city from the west without being observed would have been well-nigh impossible, even for a German. Stepping off the BEA flight at Tempelhof was akin to indecent exposure. Certainly I had cover, but this only meant I hadn't sold my memoirs to the *News of the World*. There were an awful lot of people in the business who knew who I was — a rather inconsequential member of an equally inconsequential British intelligence unit — the same way I knew a lot of them. When the opportunity arose we ate together, we drank together and, very occasionally, we killed each other. Usually this last only occurred when some interloper like Schnellinger fouled things up.

The real fly in the ointment, of course, was Roger Brookes, a man I admired and certainly didn't envy. People who thought being a motor racing driver or a steeplejack was living dangerously should have tried Brookes's job, being a double agent. Quite apart from the mental pressures there were physical hazards as well, something which had been proved when Schnellinger had ordered Klemper to pick him up. If Brookes was still alive I shuddered to think what would be happening to him.

At this point my reflections were interrupted by a knock at the door. Unhurriedly I eased myself off the bed and strolled across the room. The man standing outside bore a distinct resemblance to Lazarus before he'd had his stroke of luck; thin, gaunt and haunted, with a pallor to his skin which would have been the envy of any ten-week-old corpse.

'Hallo, Philis,' he said, his smile completing the death's-head image. The accent was immaculate New England, his origins a West Virginian mining town. 'It's great to see you again.'

'Felix,' I exclaimed jovially, shaking his hand carefully in case I broke off his arm at the shoulder. 'You are looking well.'

We sneered at each other for a moment, then I closed the door behind him and Felix started to tear the room apart in his search for bugs. I could have told him he was wasting energy he badly needed. Nothing I said to him would be of the slightest interest to anybody.

'What brings you to Berlin?' he asked once he was satisfied.

His subtlety held me spellbound. It was the direct, friendly approach, hands across the water and all that bull. Unfortunately for Felix both my hands were going to remain firmly in my pockets.

'I came to burn down the Reichstag,' I told him. 'Apparently some joker has beaten me to it.'

For a second or two we both rocked with forced laughter, only stopping when Felix went into a burst of frenzied coughing. The glass of water I fetched brought the paroxysm under control, enabling him to return to the subject uppermost on his mind.

'Seriously, though,' he said. 'What brings you to West Berlin? It's a bit off the beaten track for you.'

It was still the friendly approach, two old friends together. He was saving the pressure for later.

'I'm taking a few days' holiday,' I lied blandly. 'I'm here as an ordinary tourist.'

Felix scratched his nose thoughtfully and went over to the window to stare at the great gobs of snow drifting down outside. I lit a cigarette, waiting for stage two of the interrogation to begin. If I'd known Felix was coming I could have had the whole script written out ready for him. Or baked him a cake full of strychnine.

'I've heard you're after Schnellinger,' he said, his back turned to me.

'Why should I be interested in him?' I asked, innocence itself. 'He's your pigeon now.'

At this Felix swung round to face me. Despite his appearance he was a dangerous man to fool around with and, while his new attitude of undisguised menace didn't exactly turn my bowels to water, it didn't inspire me to do cartwheels on the carpet either.

'I've also heard you're working with a man called Sutters,' he said softly.

'But Sutters is a Russian,' I protested. 'One of those nasty Communists.'

'I know.' Felix's expression hardened perceptibly. It was the prelude to phase three, the time for a few well-chosen threats. 'Remember one thing. Any attack on Schnellinger will be regarded as a hostile act, whether it's made by the Russians or by you. Is that clear?'

'Perfectly,' I assured him.

With a grunt of approval Felix turned on his heel and made for the door. He might have nothing more to say but I had.

'What about Brookes?' I called after him.

Felix stopped with his hand on the door handle.

'Never heard of him,' he replied.

In the intelligence world there were no such things as allies.

Once Felix was safely off the premises I returned to the bed, not particularly bothered by American displeasure at my proposed course of action. It had been obvious that the Americans would be a trifle upset when they saw SR(2) lined up against them in alliance with the Russians, but, at the same time, there wasn't a great deal they could do about the situation. Even they couldn't make it open season for SR(2) agents; they could only try to protect Schnellinger. Admittedly, this in itself would have been a formidable obstacle if it hadn't been for one vital fact — the Americans were as much in the dark about Schnellinger as everybody else. They might have a monopoly of his services, but Schnellinger's whole strength lay in his anonymity. If he was brought out into the open, by anyone whomsoever, he was finished and he knew it. If the Americans managed to expose him he'd be no more than another American intelligence unit, with no independent bargaining power at all. If anyone else reached him first, the results were likely to be far more drastic. While he remained ahead of the game Schnellinger was laughing, but he'd been walking a tightrope since he'd committed himself to one power and a single slip could prove fatal. I hoped this slip had been made by Elsa Schacht.

On the dot of midnight the phone beside my bed began to ring. I made no move to lift the receiver and after half a dozen tinkles the ringing stopped. Five minutes later it rang again, only twice this time before I was left in peace. The final summons came at a quarter past the hour, eleven rings in all, and this completed the message. Klemper definitely wasn't in West Berlin, hardly surprising news, but the trip to Germany had been no wild-goose chase. At eleven o'clock the following night I should be a step nearer to Klemper and, ultimately, to Schnellinger.

This in itself was sufficient cause for satisfaction, but the knowledge Sutters was operating on schedule gave me far more, as I hadn't seen him for a couple of days. For all I knew he could have cleared off to Sakhalin. The phone calls proved he hadn't, that he'd managed to slip into West Berlin by the back door via, among other places, Dublin, Helsinki, Moscow and East Berlin. Unless something had gone very wrong nobody else who mattered should know he was in town, which put him one up over me. During the next twenty-four hours I had to go missing as well, just to even the score.

For most of the following day I was the epitome of the perfect tourist, traipsing around town and gauping at all the wonderful sights. My only consolation was that the small army keeping tabs on my movements must have been equally bored. Largely for the benefit of my unseen admirers I began with a brisk, crippling stroll in the Grunewald, not doing too well with my pretense of being entranced by the frozen, wooded wastes beside the Havel. After half an hour of this, incipient frostbite drove me back to civilization, and I spent the rest of the morning enthusiastically bombing up and down streets like the Tauentzienstrasse, Kantstrasse and Joachimstalerstrasse. It was almost as hard on my feet as on my tongue.

It was cold as well, but at first I thought it must be even worse for my shadows. They weren't allowed time for the swift, medicinal schnapps I relied on to keep me going, having to lurk in inhospitable doorways, cursing me under their breath. Just the same, although I was prepared to make life as uncomfortable as possible for them, I took good care not to lose any of my little brood. In fact, as far as I was concerned, it was the more the merrier. Nobody was likely to maltreat me with representatives of half the member countries of the United Nations in attendance.

By one o'clock what little amusement I'd derived from a conducted tour of the city had turned sour. The point I'd overlooked was that my camp followers would all be Germans, whomever they worked for. Federal Germany was still in a state of semibarbarism, a country where the workers hadn't thought of asking for the ten-minute tea breaks their British counterparts needed every hour, and my shadows were probably standing up to the exercise better than I was. Naturally, I didn't accost one of them to find out, but I did take an extended lunch break, deciding to do the rest of my sightseeing from the back seat of a taxi.

To get the afternoon off to a good start I had myself driven out of the city center, making my circuitous way into Dahlem, past the new university. Using a judicious mixture of broken German and basic English, I managed to explain what I wanted and, in course of my peregrinations, the taxi passed slowly through the Steinplatz on three separate occasions, as broad a hint as I could afford to drop.

Business disposed of, I headed back into the city, intending to have a closer look at what was possibly Europe's major tourist attraction. A man with the unlikely name of

Shih Hwang-ti had supposedly started the fashion some two hundred years B.C., both Herod and Hadrian had carried on the good work, but it had been left to one Walter Ulbricht to cap the lot, establishing himself as the top wall builder of all time. Unfortunately for him, a fair share of the perks had landed in Brandt's lap. Although the Wall had effectively cut down the flow of refugees from East Germany many of the real plums, the juicy profits, had gone to West Berlin. Fewer refugees meant the Federal German authorities could cut down on expenses for interrogations, welfare and resettlement. The Wall brought tourists flocking to West Berlin in their thousands with their welcome foreign currency, it added fuel to the morbid self-pity many Berliners seemed to thrive on and it managed to achieve this without noticeably spoiling the architecture of the city. Nothing could do this, any more than you could spoil the mill area of Pittsburgh.

Nevertheless, I found the Wall curiously impressive, both as a monument and a symbol, especially when I ascended one of the view platforms for a peek at the Vopos on the far side. My big smile and friendly wave didn't cheer them up. I only hoped they felt more hospitable come the morrow. By then, if everything went according to plan, I should be in East Berlin with them.

When I sallied forth from the hotel that night, refreshed by an early dinner and a brief stop in the bar, there must have been quite a few groans up and down the street, particularly from those in my retinue who weren't on shift work. To make it worse, from their point of view, they all knew perfectly well that I could drop them at will, however good they were at their job. The sole reason for their cold vigil was to learn exactly what I was up to and the bitter certainty that they wouldn't be there to find out couldn't have made their task any more attractive. If they had but known it, I was about to confirm their suspicions. Or so I hoped.

The manner in which this was to be achieved was as foolproof as Sutters could make it, about 102 per cent. Berlin was a city he knew and while there I was definitely cast in a supporting role, the position Sutters had held in England. With this in mind I followed his instructions to the letter. Taxi ride to the Schiller Hotel, in through the big, revolving doors, lift down to the basement garage, into the maroon Volkswagen 1600 Fastback, change overcoats, put on a ridiculous fur hat which did absolutely nothing for my image, then up, up and away. It all went like a dream. The car had lousy acceleration, and not much speed when I'd worked through the gears, but it was completely reliable and this was the only thing I was interested in. People trying to tail me by car had a mile-long drive through crowded streets before they reached the one entrance to the garage and that was only after they'd realized my intention. When they did arrive they wouldn't know whether I was in a car or on foot, my change of clothing not exactly designed to aid their subsequent search. Anybody endeavoring to follow me on foot would be in an even worse situation. The paperback edition of *A Clockwork Orange* jamming open the lift doors at basement level would slow them down more than somewhat, and the one flight of stairs was at the far side of the hotel, or so Sutters had assured me.

Once all interested parties were reconciled to having lost my trail they should start casting back in their minds to see if my previous movements gave any clue to my destination. Naturally they didn't, but, assuming everybody was on the ball, my three deliberate circuits of the Steinplatz would be recalled. My interest in the square could mean only one thing — an equal interest in Herr Klaus Winkler. The fact that all my shadows would realize I was having them on, offering one of the smelliest red herrings ever, didn't matter in the slightest. They'd still have to check the Steinplatz to make sure. Very few people had seen Winkler in the flesh, or wanted to if the photograph in his file was a good likeness, but an awful lot of influential men would recognize his voice. He was one of my personal heroes, someone who had amassed a fortune by simply sitting on his backside and waiting for the phone to ring. Part broker, part international switchboard operator, the services he rendered were so invaluable not even an idiot like Schnellinger would dare breathe heavily in his direction. There would be a lot of activity around the Steinplatz until it became apparent I was nowhere in the vicinity.

It was quite a neat ploy, the icing on the cake, but I didn't allow it to go to my head. Do that and I was likely to have it shot off, something I'd dedicated my life to avoiding. After twenty minutes' driving through the unfamiliar streets, I was lost and alone, no trace of any pursuers. Satisfied, I pulled up under a handy street sign to study my map of West Berlin. Not having had a Boy Scout training I still made a couple of wrong turns, but at a quarter past ten I was safely parked, diagonally across the road from a large apartment house on the Freistrasse.

The reasons for my visit to West Berlin were so tenuous I'd had difficulty convincing Sutters they were valid, requiring the combined archives of SR(2) and the KGB to turn them into anything resembling a lead. I certainly hadn't discovered any hard evidence at Elsa's, merely two scraps of circumstantial evidence. However, they had been sufficient for me to have a hunch and my hunches were famous, mainly because most of them were wrong. So far this had all the earmarks of being one of the lucky ones.

All I'd actually found was the flap of an envelope bearing a West Berlin post mark, plus a menu from a restaurant called Der Grosse Zeiger and, considering the amount of rubbish I'd had to sift through, it was a tribute to my eagle eye that I'd noted their significance. Sutters's initial reaction had been to suggest I'd snatched at them in sheer desperation, inventing a significance for them, but I hadn't believed him. Admittedly, the menu hadn't meant a thing when I'd first found it in the middle of a pile of correspondence and circulars. Nothing had clicked until the piece of envelope had fluttered out from the pages of the book. The postmark had no significance in itself, merely acting as a catalyst, a jog to my memory. Originally the name of Der Grosse Zeiger's proprietor hadn't consciously registered, when I saw the postmark it did and Hans Richter was a name I knew. Not just as a conductor either, although I'd been unable to place the name in its other context.

It wasn't until my phone call to Pawson the next morning that I'd been enlightened. Until four years before Richter had made his living by organizing escape routes from East Germany. Then, unaccountably, he'd retired, abandoning the underworld for the apparent security and respectability of owning a restaurant. Since then there had been no hint of subversive activity in his life. The existence of a menu from his restaurant in Elsa Schacht's living quarters couldn't be regarded as compromising, not even by the wildest stretch of the imagination, but there was an interesting coincidence involved. It was just four years before that Schnellinger had commenced operations.

As a practicing skeptic I wasn't a great believer in coincidence, so, with this as a start, it wasn't difficult to build up a working hypothesis. The one certain fact about Schnellinger was that his headquarters were located somewhere in western Europe, hidden away in some quiet backwater. He was working for the Americans, gathering information from Russia and the satellite countries among other places, and this information had to be channeled through the Iron Curtain. Given Richter's past record, it was easy to imagine how he could fit into the organization.

Unfortunately, in common with most of my hypotheses, there hadn't been a single concrete fact to support my opinion. I had enough to justify closer investigation of Richter, but not nearly enough to start treating him as an accredited Schnellinger operative. This was where Sutters came in. Moscow obviously didn't have anything on Richter — otherwise they would have dropped on him like a ton of bricks — but the Russians were having their secrets filched and Sutters could present my theory to his superiors to see if it made sense from where they sat. It had, and this had been the green light for Operation Richter. Assuming we weren't mistaken, he should make a far more promising subject for interrogation than Elsa would have been. Four years ago he had been an important man in his own right. He certainly wouldn't have joined Schnellinger as tea boy.

For half an hour I sat in the stationary car, taking frequent pulls at my hip flask and trying to convince myself I was happy in my work. It was a hard, uphill struggle. The weather might have done wonders for an Eskimo but it did nothing for me, especially as I couldn't use the car heater and the side windows had to stay down if I was to have any visibility at all through the flurries of snow. Being slowly frozen to death had always tended to depress me and it did now. When I thought of Richter my gloom only deepened. He was the one man in West Berlin, apart from Sutters, who could make an educated guess at what I was up to and he would have taken precautions. If he hadn't, matters would be even worse, meaning my Nanook of the North act was completely wasted.

Shortly after a quarter to eleven I began to forget the cold, having more important matters to occupy my mind. First of all my hip flask ran dry, cutting off the brandy supply unless a friendly Saint Bernard hove into sight. Before I could get around to cursing my enforced temperance, my attention was distracted. One moment there was only cold, wet snow coming in through the open window, the next there was also a large hairy hand with a gun. My reaction was to swallow hard, trying not to let the 9mm Browning against my left temple get me down. Although I'd heard the man creeping round the outside of the Volkswagen a good minute before, this didn't make my predicament any more enjoyable. It wasn't good for my nerves to know that an untimely squeeze from the man holding the Browning would send the inside of my head out through the far side window. Via my right ear.

'Good evening,' I said. It was a point of honor for me to be polite to men holding guns against my head. 'Can I help you?'

Of course, I could have attempted the outraged tourist bit but it wasn't worth the effort. The fellow outside hadn't stuck his gun in the ear of the first person he'd met, he'd been looking for the ear of somebody called Philis. In any case, he was no longer holding my attention, any more than the second gunman who was yanking at the locked passenger door. My eyes were on a pedestrian walking in our direction on the far pavement. I recognized him at once despite the seventy-five yards separating him from the car, the terrible visibility and the short time we'd been acquainted. It wasn't merely the fact that he'd hit me over the head on the one occasion we'd met which jogged my memory. I'd had a clear view of his face when he passed beneath a streetlamp and, as a keen geography student, I knew there were a lot more Chinamen to be found in Peking than in the Freistrasse, West Berlin.

Of a sudden I was again concentrating exclusively on the gun. It had been pushed a foot farther inside the car, my head, of necessity, going with it. A face had joined the Browning and the arm in the window, a bearded face with a nasty look in its eye.

'Open the passenger door,' it said in gutteral English, the split of the mouth in the beard revealing a set of neglected teeth.

The breath coming out wasn't anything to write home about either, but I wasn't his best friend so I didn't mention it, preferring to do exactly as I'd been told. Although, since spotting the Chinaman, I'd lost what little enthusiasm I'd had for the original plan, the cold metal pressing against my head meant that, for the moment, I didn't have much option. Richter should be returning from Der Grosse Zeiger in less than fifteen minutes, so this was how long I had to ditch two armed killers and warn Sutters that Chinese minds had been working along the same devious lines as our own. This had always been in the cards, especially as Joyce had appropriated my wallet in Nottingham, but we had banked on being a day or two ahead. Now I knew better.

Nottingham, England, January 1972

The discovery of the body of Mrs. O'Malley, the woman Klemper had once known as Elsa Schacht, was largely fortuitous. Her corpse might have remained hidden for days if it hadn't been for a sudden shower of rain which had interrupted the late-night farewells of a teen-age couple.

'Let's go across the road,' the boy had suggested.

He'd indicated a row of unoccupied houses, all of them scheduled for demolition.

'There might be rats,' his girl friend had objected, buttoning her raincoat over her disheveled clothing.

A sudden increase in the intensity of the rain persuaded her to change her mind. Little more than five minutes after they had entered one of the derelict buildings, the whole neighborhood was aroused by the girl's hysterical screams when she discovered what lay beneath the pile of old sacks they had been about to use as a makeshift bed.

8

THE WAY RICHTER'S TAME HEAVIES eased themselves into the Fastback didn't encourage me to assume that they'd willingly allow me to walk out of their lives in a quarter of an hour. Rather, they gave me the impression that when we went our separate ways my bullet-riddled body would have been dumped in the Havel, probably with a mixture of old chains and concrete to keep me company. Gunman number one kept the Browning against my head while his companion clambered into the back seat, then gunman number two massaged the back of my neck with his gun until the fellow with the beard joined me in the front.

'You're sure you've got the right man?' I asked hopefully.

There was no immediate reply, the man beside me far too busy going through my pockets. When he'd finished he showed his appreciation by punching me in the teeth. Hard. The gun boring into my neck persuaded me not to retaliate, and I contented myself with spitting a mouthful of blood through the window before I shut it.

'You haven't a gun?'

It was the man with the beard again, sounding taken aback.

'What would I need a gun for? I'm here on holiday.'

The only answer was a grunt. A quick search of the

likely hiding places didn't produce anything, hardly surprising as I didn't have a gun, not in the car at any rate.
For the first time the man in the back spoke. The speech
was in German and, as a natural linguist, I couldn't understand much he said. His companion was happy to act as
interpreter.

'Where's Sutters?' he demanded.

'I don't know,' I answered, more or less honestly.

A large, unfriendly hand dropped into my lap, my head
went forward against the windshield and I practiced a
falsetto scream until the gun caught up with the back of
my neck.

'Where's Sutters?'

'I promised not to tell,' I said shakily, 'but you've persuaded me. He's gone to visit his sick mother in Tashkent.'

Though his heart wasn't really in it, the man with the
beard thumped me in the face yet again, adding fuel to the
active dislike I was developing. After ten wasted minutes
he was beginning to realize a parked car wasn't the place to
persuade me to open my heart. For a few seconds my captors shot rapid-fire German at one another while I rested
my aching head on the cool glass of the windshield, not
particularly interested in their discussion. Then the one
in the back grabbed me by the hair and jerked me upright.

'We're going for a ride,' my friend with the beard informed me.

'Great,' I muttered automatically.

It was about time unless my timetable was to go right up
the spout.

Following instructions to the letter, I started up and began
driving carefully through the slush. The Volkswagen had

been as cold as a tomb before we set out, but after ten minutes there was still no reaction from my passengers and I was becoming desperate. I was on the point of acting off my own bat when the man beside me finally broke.

'Isn't there a heater?' he inquired.

My heart warmed to him and it was a crying shame he'd never know what a good question he'd asked. To make matters absolutely perfect we were running through a residential district, houses set well back from the road and no traffic worth talking about. Eager to oblige, I took as deep a breath as I could manage without making this too obvious before I put the heater switch full on. Thirty seconds later I pushed it back to cold, slammed on the brakes and stumbled out into the bitter night air. Even though I'd been holding my breath my legs weren't at all steady and I leant against the fender for a couple of minutes until there was nothing except pure air being pumped through my respiratory system.

This left me with another four minutes to kill before it would be safe to reenter the car, and I used the time to retrieve the gun somebody had thoughtfully placed in the trunk at the front. Satisfied that it was in working order, and that the blast of cold air would have flushed out the interior of the Volkswagen, I climbed into the car where the two Germans were sleeping like babies. Dead babies, that is. Chemical warfare might be frowned upon by all civilized countries, but it had proved impossible to stifle the spirit of the scientific research and PXC was the brain-child of a bunch of humanitarians in the Urals. Reading the dry, statistical report on its properties had been frightening enough. Seeing it kill two fully grown, healthy human beings in a little over twenty seconds had decided me it would take a hell of a lot of provocation to make me declare war on the U.S.S.R.

Circumspect wasn't the word to describe my return to the Freistrasse. For the first part of the journey, after I'd dumped the bodies in the snow, I could have been a competitor in one of the special stages of the Monte Carlo rally, frightening even myself as I pushed the Volkswagen to the limit of its performance on the treacherous roads. This was mainly for show because, however fast I went, I was going to be too late to take part in what had to be happening in Richter's apartment. Once I was in shooting distance of the Freistrasse I abandoned the heroics, which were out of character, and resorted to total discretion. Of course, I could be wrong, everything might have gone just as Sutters had anticipated. It could be that the Chinaman, the same one who had coshed me in Nottingham, was in Berlin on business completely unconnected with Richter, had taken his evening constitutional along the Freistrasse purely by chance. For Sutters's sake I would have liked this to have been the case, the same way I would have liked to have won half a million on the Pools or to have had the sex appeal of Rudolf Valentino. I made Sutters a distinct outsider and all my money would have been on the Chinese to have the situation in hand.

My sedate drive down the Freistrasse did nothing to disprove this theory, although there was nothing to substantiate it either. In keeping with my heartfelt desire not to advertise my presence, I drove straight past the apartment building, maintaining a steady cruising speed designed to indicate due regard for the prevailing icy conditions without suggesting particular interest in Richter's domicile.

Two hundred yards down the road I turned left into a side street, then took the first right before finding a place to park.

The basic disadvantage of attempting to conceal my interest in Richter was that I'd been traveling too fast to see very much, only that the lights were switched on in Richter's third-floor apartment and that there was a man loafing inconspicuously in the hallway of the building. This wasn't much but at least it was something. The lights told me I was definitely too late, that Richter was back from the restaurant, and the man lurking in the doorway meant there had been no mass exodus as yet. He also had another significance. Although I couldn't be sure whether Richter or the Chinese had ended on top, the presence of a sentry was proof positive that Sutters was up to his neck in something or other.

Absolutely nothing about the situation inspired me to blunder in brandishing my trusty Colt. Slowly and methodically I thought the problem through, painfully aware of the precious seconds ticking away, something which paled into insignificance when balanced against my even more precious well-being. In order to postpone facing the grisly truth for as long as possible, I generously allowed myself three alternatives. The one I favored most involved getting the hell out of the area, having a few drinks in a suitable bar and hauling some nubile scrubber back to the hotel. Residual pride, plus a certain uneasiness about how Pawson and the Russians might view such a move, persuaded me this wasn't really on. My second choice, calling in reinforcements, wasn't much better. The idea of having some support had distinct appeal but this would take far too long to organize. Felix was the only person I could

think of who was likely to respond quickly and unques-
tioningly to an appeal for help, and it was hard to visualize him arranging any form of rescue bid for my benefit.

All this left me exactly where I didn't want to be —
walking into the building brandishing my trusty Colt.
The prospect was enough to make a confirmed kamikaze
think twice, and when I hauled myself out of the car it was
with a certain lack of enthusiasm. For their own sake I
hoped the residents of the district went to bed early. I had
no way of knowing how many people had entered Richter's
apartment, but I had a feeling there would be a smaller
number coming out and I was totally committed to the
policy of being one of them. To achieve this laudable aim
I was prepared to treat everyone as an enemy once I was
inside the building, bar none. Nuns, women with child,
old-age pensioners, they'd all have to take their chances if
they were in my way.

The snow was blowing directly in my face as I walked
along the Freistrasse, my coat collar turned up and the
ridiculous fur hat jammed low on my forehead. However,
my chattering teeth and goose pimples weren't solely the
product of cold. Philis was scared, with a gut-wrenching
fear which not only proved I was healthy and sane but gave
me a life expectancy twice that of the average hero. Not
that the sentry I'd spotted from the car bothered me, he
was the least of my worries. Standing where he was made
him a sitting duck, someone to be gunned down whenever
I felt like it. Just the same I walked straight past him,
head averted, without even a muttered '*Guten Abend,*'
hoping I looked more like an honest, law-abiding burgher
than the silly one I felt. The cigarette end I'd seen glow-

ing in a doorway on the far side of the street, not to mention the man I'd passed who was sitting at the wheel of a parked Mercedes, told me it was neither the time nor the place to start a shooting war. With at least three men patrolling the street, the Chinese operation made Sutters's plan seem pretty sick.

Even so I didn't consider giving up for a second. Instead I gave the idea my devoted attention for the full five minutes it took me to stroll past Richter's building and enter the door of the apartment block on the far side. Pleasantly relieved to have come in from the cold, I lit a cigarette, relying on the nicotine to help my thought processes. There were other entrances to the building next door but it wasn't worth the effort to check them. If there were three men littering up the Freistrasse I couldn't imagine the back door would be left unattended. This being the case, the only way I could think of to reach my objective made me regard my original plan with nostalgic regret.

Luckily the building possessed an elevator because what I had to do was dangerous enough without tiring myself out by scrambling up endless flights of stairs. I did have a few steps to climb as the top floor was the tenth and I was going higher still, but by this time I was in no great hurry.

The roof, as expected, wasn't exactly overcrowded. There was me, some clotheslines, the building housing the elevator mechanism, two large storage tanks, a few television aerials and a hell of a lot of snow. Down at street level it had been snowing hard, ten stories up there was a full-fledged blizzard, ideal conditions for broad jumping. Back in my schooldays, when I'd been young, fit and eager to impress the female spectators, I'd managed a leap of

around twenty feet at the school sports. Assuming I repeated this performance now, I'd still be left some ten feet
short of my objective and the odd hundred feet above
ground level, even before I allowed for the parapets running round both roofs. Nor did the man on the roof next
door make things any easier.

I went down behind the parapet as fast as gravity and
fear permitted, wondering what I'd done to annoy the
fellow running affairs up above. The wisdom of my move
was proved a fraction of a second later when something
slapped against the far side of the parapet. The Americans
were busily manufacturing side-arm ammunition which
fired right through brick walls, but the man next door had
forgotten to bring any with him, which was just fine by
me. For a couple of minutes I lay in the snow, getting cold
and wet and trying to think how I could regain the safety
of the building without stopping a couple of bullets in the
back. Although the visibility was terrible, theoretically a
point in my favor, I wasn't reassured. To leave the roof I
had to pass through the one and only door, and inside the
lights were on. I knew precisely what I would have done
in the unknown gunman's position and, unless my adver-
sary had an epileptic fit or a mental blackout, I didn't give
myself one chance in a thousand. This was when I looked
on the bright side.

Apparently the gunman enjoyed shooting for the sake of
it as there was a second slap against the concrete of the
parapet, then something brushed against my arm. This
was when I realized no one was shooting at me. Unlike
boomerangs, bullets couldn't travel round corners and, for
the life of me, I couldn't imagine why anyone should try
to kill me by throwing lengths of clothesline.

Keeping a firm hold on the frayed end of the rope, I

pushed myself out of the snow, intent on finding something to tie it to. After I'd settled for the thickest of the
pipes leading from what looked like a water tank, I gave
my devoted attention to tying some of the securest knots
ever. Satisfied nothing was likely to slip my end, I did my
best to check the knots on the roof next door, pulling hard
on the line. Although nothing broke I still wasn't finished.
The line might be thin, strong rope but my weight was
going to rub it against the edge of the parapet, something
which might prove fatal. A hundred feet of free fall didn't
appeal to me, not when I knew I didn't bounce.

Once the vital area of the balustrade was safely padded
with handfuls of compressed snow I'd run out of excuses
for delay. Everybody was entitled to one pet phobia and it
was unfortunate mine happened to be heights. Suspend a
similar clothesline four feet above the ground and I could
probably travel half a mile in complete safety. Put it at
the top of a ten-story building and covering a distance of
ten yards or so became as easy as swimming the Atlantic.

Bravery wasn't a commodity I'd ever classified but swinging myself over the parapet was the bravest thing I wanted
to do. And something I regretted immediately. Hanging
upside down on a thin, sagging rope a hundred feet up,
buffeted by the wind, my hands numbed with cold, was far
worse than I'd visualized. My only answer was to empty
my mind of everything except the directives to my hands
and feet which would see me to the far side in one piece.
An eternity later, when my feet touched the opposite
parapet, my whole body was drenched with sweat, my
metabolism defying the elements and the overcoat I'd had
to leave behind, and I was glad Sutters was there to help
me up on to the roof. I think he was quite pleased to see
me as well, although, naturally, he didn't say so.

'You should be dead,' I said, the cold of the roof exchanged for the relative warmth of the stairs inside.

'I'm sorry to disappoint you.'

Sutters was grinning, looking disgustedly cheerful considering what faced us, and this worried me. The length of clothesline swinging nonchalantly from his right hand worried me some more. Come to that, I couldn't think of anything concerning our situation which didn't worry me.

'I thought you might need someone to hold your hand,' he explained.

We were standing just inside the door leading from the roof, our voices low. Unless I'd remembered the five years or so spent hanging in space, I could have been forgiven for thinking I'd returned to my starting point. Everything, from the burnt orange of the walls to the numbers on the doors, was exactly the same.

'You'd better put me in the picture,' I suggested.

John grinned again, increasing my unease. He gave every indication of belonging to the rare breed of people who thrived on the prospect of danger. He was good, his record proved this, but now I suspected he was dangerous to work with. One day he was likely to take a completely unnecessary risk and I didn't want this to happen while I was around.

'There isn't a great deal to tell,' Sutters began, unaware he'd been on my portable psychiatrist's couch. 'I saw you draw off the two outriders and I was all set to take Richter and his personal bodyguard. Then Joyce and his friends arrived and I thought I'd better stay out of the way until I knew what I was up against.'

'Joyce is here then?'

'In person. I thought the news would please you.'

For the record it didn't, but I let the remark pass.

'How many altogether?' I asked.

'Eight, but Joyce and the Chinaman are the only real danger. The rest are just local help. They won't stay long once the shooting starts.''

He made everything appear so simple I wondered why I hadn't left him to deal with the situation alone.

'Where are they all? I've seen the three in the Frei-strasse.'

'There's a man at each of the other two entrances,' Sutters told me. 'Joyce, the Chinaman and one other man are with Richter. They're using drugs so there's no desper-ate rush. They should be busy for another hour yet.'

His confidence still hadn't infected me. If we wanted Richter we had to go in after him. The way I saw it no one was going to open the front door and invite us in.

'I take it you have everything worked out,' I said a trifle bitterly.

'More or less,' Sutters admitted.

He looked as though he was likely to burst out laughing at any moment.

'And does the clothesline play some part in your strategy?'

'It does,' Sutters answered, his face all smiles. 'I know you enjoy jumping through windows, and after the way you shinned across from the building next door I thought you might fancy an encore.'

The only thing wrong with the idea Sutters proceeded to outline was that I couldn't dream up anything better. Objectively, I had to admit his proposal offered us the best chance of snatching Richter before Joyce disposed of him. Subjectively, I felt a great repugnance for my assigned role. The whole operation hinged on two factors — total surprise and the empty apartment above Richter's. With five sentries posted, Joyce wouldn't be expecting unannounced visitors, certainly not through the window.

Apart from the furnishings the empty flat on the fourth floor was an identical twin to Richter's apartment below. The outside door opened directly into a sizable lounge, running the entire width of the apartment and ending at the double windows which overlooked the street. All the other rooms lay to the left — kitchen, bedrooms, bathroom, et cetera. As Joyce was conducting Richter's interrogation in the living room, this was the only one of interest.

On this occasion a heavy sofa, weighted down with the contents of a couple of bookcases, served to secure one end of the rope. Before exiting through the window, however, I had to wait until Sutters had taken the bad shoulder I envied him to the floor below, and I used the time to check my gun. In any case, quite apart from my dislike of heights, I wanted to postpone leaving for as long as possible. While I'd been cavorting about at rooftop level nobody in the street could possibly have seen me. Outside the lighted windows of Richter's apartment I was almost certain to be spotted and I didn't relish the idea of people taking potshots at me.

Exactly four minutes after Sutters had started down the stairs, I dropped the rope out of the window, offered brief prayers to every deity from Allah to Zoroaster and went out myself. It was only a few feet to the sill below and I covered them fast. Resting there, gun in hand and pressed as far to one side of the window as possible, I could hear no immediate sounds of excitement from the street. There was only the murmur of people speaking German inside Richter's apartment, one voice brisk and authoritative, that of an interrogator, the other slow, stumbling and confused, the voice of a man who had been drugged. Not with heroin or with anything like that, but with one of the specialist drugs which made people confess to their dirty underwear and personal habits. This state of affairs lasted for only a few seconds, then all manner of interesting things began to happen, events which would have been incomprehensible to anyone not expecting them. There was a series of soft, thunking explosions, the tinkle of breaking glass, exclamations of surprise, the noise of sudden movement, a thud as something heavy hit the floor. I knew exactly what had happened because it was my cue. While Joyce and company were wondering who had emptied a silenced automatic through the front door, I intended to surprise them a bit more.

Moving sideways to the middle of the window, I did two practice swings, pushing off from the sill to build up momentum, before I straightened my legs and drove in at the center pane. I was lucky. Either of the two shots from the street might have hit me, I might have bounced off the glass or I might have become hopelessly entangled in the curtains. At it was I couldn't have hoped for a better entry. My feet exploded through the glass as if it hadn't been there and, when I released the rope, I landed on a clear patch of carpet instead of crashing into a piece of furniture.

Even so there was no hope of immediately steadying into a firing position and I rolled away to my left, finishing flat on my stomach and facing the door. This wasted a fraction of a second but I had it in hand. When I drifted in through the window, the people inside, those who were still alive, had had less than fifteen seconds to adjust to the barrage through the front door, and my spectacular entrance had thrown them into mental chaos. Joyce, standing out of line of any more shots through the door, managed one bullet at the shattered window as I began to roll, a second shot at the spot where I'd landed as I brought up my gun, and took two bullets in the chest before his hand and brain were fully synchronized. The Chinaman, the only other member of the opposition still standing and hampered by a bullet wound in his side, was even slower. He was bending to retrieve his gun from the carpet when I shot him, straightening him into the path of the bullet Sutters fired as he came in. The Chinaman somersaulted over the back of the sofa, leaving a slimy trail of blood behind him, and this just about closed the proceedings. The other of Joyce's men lay where he'd been since I'd arrived, the spreading stain beneath him suggesting he was a poor insurance risk.

Up on my feet, I examined the shambles the room had become. What with the great hunks of plaster gouged from the walls, the shattered glass, the ruined furniture and the three dead or dying bodies, it no longer resembled a living room. Some firm of interior decorators stood to make a fortune restoring the place to normality, but I had no intention of being there when they arrived. While Sutters made the rounds to insure Joyce and his men didn't get to talk to anyone, I went across the Richter. He was sitting slackly in an armchair, his back half-turned to the door, and it seemed the drug had knocked him out completely. He certainly wasn't paying much attention to the proceedings. On closer examination he didn't look at all healthy, his skin waxy white, not even the shallowest breathing to show he was alive. With my hand inside his jacket and over his heart I could still find no signs of life, just something warm and sticky to the touch. Displaying remarkable restraint I walked round the armchair to have a look at the bullet hole in the back.

'You stupid sod,' I said to Sutters. 'You've killed Richter.'

Villa Rosa, Spain, January 1972

'How is the Englishman today?' Klemper asked.

Brookes lay on the bed, head bandaged, left leg in plaster, listening as the two men discussed him, referring to him as though he were a favorite pet. They could ignore him, pretend he wasn't there, but Brookes didn't mind. He knew that when Klemper began to question him directly the end would be very near.

'He's as well as can be expected,' said the doctor, a fussy little martinet of a man who found Klemper's incessant queries irritated him immeasurably. 'I practice medicine, not miracles.'

'How long before he'll be up and about?'

Other people's irritation had no effect on Klemper.

'I can't say exactly,' the doctor answered, carefully replacing instruments in his medical bag. 'He certainly won't be fit to leave his bed for another two weeks.'

Klemper nodded and followed the doctor out of the door, leaving Brookes alone with Hans. The two of them had, of necessity, established a working relationship. If ordered to do so, Hans would kill Brookes unhesitatingly and, given the opportunity, Brookes would have returned the compliment with an equal lack of compunction. Accepting this as said, they went out of their way to be friendly, to live side by side without grating on each other's nerves.

'Give me a cigarette,' Brookes said.

'After what the doctor said?' Hans replied, his pallid, moon face splitting into a smile.

He produced a pack of Bisonte from his pocket, lit two and handed one to Brookes. For a minute they both smoked in silence.

'You're all right for a fortnight,' Hans commented suddenly, putting Brookes's thoughts into words.

Klemper was an advocate of British justice when it suited him, the kind that had existed prior to the abolition of capital punishment. He nursed his prisoners back to health before he obliterated them.

9

Richter's death was a bitter blow. He would certainly have been able to help us locate Klemper, if not Schnellinger, but with his death we were back at square one. Moreover, however favorable the light, Sutters and I didn't emerge with flying colors. If we were considered purely as executioners we'd been doing a grand job, butchering people left, right and center. The drawback was that, apart from Richter, whom we'd wanted alive anyway, the men we'd killed were hardly worth the waste of ammunition. All we'd achieved was to cut down Schnellinger's overheads by decimating his hired help. Although the exposure and elimination of Joyce was something of a feather in my cap, I didn't expect much praise from Pawson. He'd point out, quite correctly, that this was a side issue, that I'd merely been doing DI5's dirty work for them. All in all it added up to a black mark on my file, almost as big as the one against Sutters's name in Moscow. Furthermore, with Richter's death, the Anglo-Russian entente was over and unlikely to be revived.

This was what led to the trouble in East Berlin, the real hard core of my anger. Once we'd discovered Richter was mortuary bound neither Sutters nor I had been tempted to stay on the premises. Our little contretemps in Richter's apartment had roused half the neighborhood, and we had no intention of waiting for a chat with the police. We didn't say much to each other either, not even when we were in the car, both of us flat with reaction and disappointment. It had been left to Sutters to voice our feelings.

'I suppose we've done our bit to liven up West Berlin,' he remarked.

'It's been a fun evening, all right,' I agreed bitterly. 'At least the Saint Valentine's Day massacre had some point in it.'

For a moment or two we were silent as we watched two police vans, sirens blaring, drive past in the other direction.

'Where do we go from here?' I asked when I could no longer see them in the driving mirror. 'Do we split up?'

'It looks like it,' Sutters answered. 'There's no reason to stick together when we're at a dead end. We can always join forces again if either of us comes up with something.'

Although I nodded, it was with total lack of conviction. The alliance had been one of expediency alone. Now, without necessarily being hostile, SR(2) and the KGB would be seeking their own ways to Schnellinger, each hoping to beat the other, and it was unlikely there would be any further cooperation. What I hadn't banked on was the way Sutters's mind was working.

Entering East Berlin posed no real problems. Naturally, we couldn't sail blithely through Checkpoint Charlie, but traffic under the Wall ran in both directions and it was much easier to defect from west to east than vice versa. We abandoned the Fastback a quarter of a mile from our destination, covering the rest of the distance to the small antique shop on foot. Once there we stayed long enough for me to be blindfolded, then we were on our way again in another car, person unknown at the wheel. After a ten-minute drive Sutters helped me from the car and into a building, its musty smell indicating disuse. There was the sound of a trap door being lifted, I was guided down some steps, the trap door was replaced above my head and then Sutters removed the blindfold. We were in a tunnel, roughly bricked at the sides, which stretched far beyond the beam of the flashlight Sutters had acquired somewhere along the route. When Sutters began walking I followed, not wanting to be left all alone in the dark.

At the other end, a good half mile according to my calculations, the same process was repeated in reverse, the only variation being that I had the blindfold removed in the car. This didn't imply any lapse in security as all the back windows of the Zil were blacked out. Just the same, I was genuinely amused when I grinned at Sutters. If I ever felt vindictive enough I could find the West Berlin entrance to the tunnel, blindfold or no blindfold.

This was the last occasion I smiled for a fortnight. The building we were taken to reeked of officialdom, Russo-German style, with plenty of uniforms and hardware in evidence. Our guide conducted us through a maze of drab, olive-painted corridors to our objective, a canteen redolent with the exotic smell of stale cabbage and overcooked potatoes. A chubby, kindly-looking man was awaiting us there, dressed in the uniform of a colonel in the Soviet Army. Without being introduced, I identified him as Mikhail Alexei Raskin, one of the Russians' chief liaison officers in East Germany. According to reputation he was about as kindly as a hungry boa constrictor.

Nevertheless, Sutters and Raskin seemed pleased to see

each other, following a warm embrace with an excited exchange in Russian. Latin languages were my speciality, my Russian being severely restricted, and I was rather out of things, not really sharing the general enthusiasm. It wasn't that I didn't like to watch the reunion of old friends, just that I didn't wholly appreciate the amused glances being thrown in my direction. For the life of me, I couldn't remember doing anything amusing during the past few hours.

Eventually Raskin decided he wasn't fulfilling his role as gracious host, leaving Sutters and coming over to shake my hand.

'It's a pleasure to meet you, Philis,' he said, speaking English as though his mouth was full of broken glass. 'I'll do everything in my power to make your stay as comfortable as possible.'

I was still mulling over the implications of the word 'stay' when Sutters broke in with a smile.

'I'm afraid I have to leave,' he told me. 'There's a plane waiting. Mikhail is arranging a flight for you tomorrow, probably to Copenhagen.'

Halfheartedly I went through the motions of bidding Sutters a fond farewell. Although both men were friendly enough, they gave the impression of sharing a joke together. I had an uncomfortable premonition that it might be at my expense, and I was beginning to wish I'd taken my chances in West Berlin, not come under the Wall.

With Sutters gone Colonel Raskin, as promised, really put himself out to make me feel at home. The meal he provided certainly wasn't ordinary canteen fare, the wine was French, the cigars were Cuban and the coffee was good enough to have been Colombian. To top it off, Raskin himself was excellent company, steering well clear of any potentially contentious topics, and I went to bed in a comfortable room on the top floor with my suspicions temporarily dispelled.

After the strenuous activities of the previous night I slept well and it was nearly eleven o'clock when I awoke. Leisurely I dressed and shaved, then decided to hunt round for a cup of coffee, my ambition cruelly aborted by the locked door. Thoughtfully I returned to the bed. It was possible Raskin didn't want me wandering about in what was obviously a headquarters building, a reasonable enough attitude, or there could be a more sinister motive. Whatever the reason I wasn't likely to learn the answer by exercising my buttocks on the edge of the bed, so I pressed the hospital-type bellpush. Service was fast, so fast, in fact, that I was tempted to think in terms of a guard posted outside the door, a theory which was supported by the red-flashed uniform and skeleton-grip machine pistol of the man who answered my call. On the other hand, if I was a prisoner the gun I had in my shoulder holster didn't make much sense.

I was still endeavoring to rationalize the situation when we reached the canteen. This time there were a dozen or more people there, a mixture of civilians and military personnel, Russians and East Germans, but I was sociably seated in a corner by myself. Another difference was in the quality of the fare offered to me. I rejected a portion of mutated black pudding, decided I wasn't likely to get any corn flakes and settled for a pot of coffee with the consistency of liquid mud. The label on the packet probably said WEHRMACHT ERSATZ SURPLUS. Absorbed with the problem of whether it was preferable to die of thirst or risk a second cup, I wasn't aware of Raskin until he'd nearly reached my table.

'I trust you slept well,' he said jovially as he sat down opposite me.

'Like the dead,' I quipped, deciding against the second coffee. 'Have you been able to arrange a flight?'

Raskin shrugged repentantly before he answered.

'I'm afraid not,' he told me with no noticeable regret. 'It's rather difficult at the moment. There's a heavy fog at the airport and no planes can take off.'

'That is unfortunate,' I said politely.

The fog must have been strictly localized because there was a pale, watery sun shining outside the canteen windows. In the same way, I now knew I hadn't heard any planes pass over the building since I'd woken, just half a dozen high-flying cars.

'When is the fog likely to clear?' I inquired.

'It's hard to say. Sometimes the visibility doesn't improve for a fortnight at a time.'

Raskin's smile remained unanswered. Fair enough, from his point of view it was absolutely hilarious and, wherever he was, Sutters would be laughing himself sick. I faced a fortnight twiddling my thumbs in East Berlin while Sutters got on with the job of locating Schnellinger, two weeks in which I'd be completely out of touch with London. Not that I'd be a prisoner, despite the locked doors and armed guards. This would be a breach of the agreement Pawson and I had negotiated with Petrov. I wouldn't be searched, I wouldn't be questioned and all my creature comforts would be catered for, probably including female companionship if I so desired. The one snag was that there wasn't a hope in hell of my leaving East

Berlin before Raskin decided to let me go, before he played God and blew away the fog.

The sight of Peter Collins waiting in the Customs hall at Heathrow didn't particularly cheer me up. His presence meant I enjoyed uninterrupted progress out of the airport, but it also meant an immediate meeting with Pawson, something I could have done without for a year or two.

'Any chance of a drink on the way?' I asked once Peter had maneuvered his car onto the open road.

'Not unless I want my head beside yours on the chopping block, which I don't,' Peter answered. 'In case you hadn't guessed, you're no longer Pawson's blue-eyed boy.'

The news came as no great surprise, no more than my reception at SR(2) headquarters. Everyone I saw greeted me with the kind of smug amusement which indicated they knew I was about to receive a rocket. The one exception was Miss Sherwood, who greeted me so effusively, in a manner not at all in keeping with her secretarial status, that I decided I could definitely forgive her her relationship with Pawson. I would far rather have stayed with her, fostering a deeper understanding, than traipsed upstairs to see Pawson. It only needed him to ask where I'd been hiding for the past fortnight and he was heading for a broken nose.

'Where the hell have you been hiding for the last two weeks?' Pawson barked once his office door was closed behind me.

Mentally I flattened his nose before throwing him out of the window, then I sat down and lit a cigarette.

'Where the hell do you think I've been?' I asked in a tone every bit as pleasant as the one Pawson had used. 'On holiday at Butlin's?'

'I asked you a serious question.'

Pawson's voice had softened and he was leaning slightly forward, sure-fire signs that he was really angry. Far angrier than he had any right to be. Another of his operations must be fouled up and he was using me as an all-purpose whipping boy. It was my turn to lean forward.

'Mr. Pawson, sir,' I said. 'Either we discuss this in a civilized manner or you can take a running jump. The choice is yours.'

For a long moment Pawson glared at me at a range of less than a foot, then the ice in his eyes thawed and he actually smiled. Every so often he liked to prove he still belonged with the rest of humanity.

'All right, I'll give you the benefit of the doubt,' he conceded. 'What was the problem?'

He rose to his feet, moving toward his cache of liquor, and I relaxed. Pawson owed it to his position to try to establish his authority and I owed it to myself to resist. Now that we'd settled for a hard-fought draw I could tell him exactly what had happened in Berlin. I wouldn't suffer for my insubordination until later.

Our discussion lasted a good two hours, and when I eventually reached my flat I was ready for a long evening with a bottle of something strong. The sackload of correspondence on the doormat was a testimony to my wide range of friends and acquaintances, comprising a telephone bill, two circulars and a letter with a Spanish stamp, not much of a haul considering the length of time I'd been away. Before I could open any of the envelopes I was disturbed, the knock at the door coming while I was still running through the list of people I knew who could write and might be in Spain.

'Haven't you got a home of your own?' I asked Henry Tate. Then I noticed the bottle he was carrying and invited him in.

Tate might be in his dotage, on the verge of retirement, but his thirty years in intelligence had given him the almost feminine trait of examining his surroundings down to the last speck of dust. While I drifted round collecting glasses and broaching the bottle of Gordon's, he tore my living room apart with his eyes, noting everything from the pile of letters I'd left on the table to the titles of the books on the shelves. I wished him good luck but his presence worried me. The head of DI5 didn't come visiting without a very good reason.

'What's the bribe for?' I asked, indicating the bottle of gin.

'It's a mark of appreciation.'

It was difficult to stop myself from sneering so I didn't bother. Although Tate was undoubtedly grateful for the exposure of Joyce, he'd be far less pleased by the knowledge that he'd been exposed by a member of another department. It was the kind of thing which looked bad on the record.

'You've heard Joyce is dead?' I inquired.

'Of course. I take it you had a hand in his death.'

'I did, and that should be worth a crate of champagne at the very least. Just think of the time and money I've saved you.'

Preferring to present the act as a disinterested gesture of friendship, I neglected to mention that if I hadn't shot Joyce he would have done me irreparable harm. Tate merely smiled enigmatically and sipped his gin without comment. Any second he'd come to the real reason for his visit.

'It seems as though there's a regular treasure hunt for Schnellinger,' he remarked casually.

I treated him to a noncommittal grunt.

'Have you made much progress?'

There was no reason why I should answer him as he was no longer likely to tell the police who had arranged Sutters's escape. On the other hand, all the information I could give him was of the negative variety, of no use to anyone.

'Not really,' I told him. 'We've had a duck shoot of his underlings but that's as far as it goes. We're further from Schnellinger than we were when we started.'

'Really?'

Tate didn't believe me.

'That's right. At the moment we don't have a thing to go on.'

Tate still didn't believe me but, rather surprisingly, he didn't press the point. Instead he contented himself with another glass of gin and some small chat to prove he hadn't come to pump me about progress in the Schnellinger case. To be polite I lent myself to the charade, not being over-communicative in case Tate was tempted to stay. Evidently he didn't consider a conversation with me as one of the highlights of his life, taking less than a quarter of an hour to decide he had to go. Somehow I managed to hold back the tears and saw him out before I returned to the interrupted chore of opening my mail.

The letter from Spain was the one which intrigued me and I opened it first, only to find it was hardly worth the effort. It was precisely the kind of letter I would have expected from someone fortunate enough to be wintering in San Antonio Abad. There was mention of the wonderful weather to make me even more aware of the hard frost and slush outside, ecstatic comments on the cheap food and wine to make me brood about the British cost of living and a wish-you-were-here which could be interpreted as a belly laugh at my misfortune at being stuck in London. The signature at the end didn't mean a thing until I glanced at the enclosed photograph and associated the name Julie with the girl who'd briefly shared both my flat and my bed. In the photograph she was wearing a skimpy bikini but she held my attention for no more than a fraction of a second, only until I recognized one of the faces in the background.

The shock of recognition was so great the photograph slipped from my fingers, a piece of clumsiness which indubitably saved my life. I hadn't bent far when the machine gunner across the street opened fire, but it was enough to insure I merely lost an inessential sliver of flesh from the back of my neck instead of being decapitated. The attack was so unexpected and so short in duration there was no time for conscious thought, less than two seconds separating the first shot from the last. The bullet which grazed my neck must have been one of the first half dozen and none of the others touched me, but this didn't make the man with a Czech M61 any less of an expert. Lying on the floor in the deafening silence following the two-second burst, I could see every one of the twenty rounds in his clip had hit a section of wall no more than a yard square, despite the fact he'd been on automatic. If I hadn't been bending when he started to fire, no one would have been able to make a death mask of me, not unless he was good at jigsaw puzzles.

When Tate burst into the room I was still lying on the carpet, head turned away from the window, still cringing in case my would-be assassin used a second clip to make sure I was dead. Taking in the devastation area the room had become, the blood pouring from my neck and the gun I had pointing at the door, half-concealed beneath my body, Tate's mouth opened on the questions you ask some-one who's just survived a machine-gunning. I interrupted him fast.

'Don't say anything, Henry,' I said urgently, before he had a chance to get started. 'Just lock the door, then come and examine my body.'

The complete professional, Tate swallowed his inquisi-tiveness and went to deal with the door. Once we were safe from interruption he knelt beside me, dabbing at the blood on my neck to make sure it wasn't tomato sauce and taking my pulse. While he imitated Dr. Kildare I told him what I wanted done, paying no heed to the uproar outside.

'The character with the machine gun must think he nailed me,' I began, 'and I don't want to disillusion him. Use your little green card to stop the police from reaching me. I'll lie here until you can contact Pawson and have him send his ambulance unit to carry me out in style.'

Without a word Tate went off to do as I'd asked, leaving me alone with my thoughts. Mainly I wanted to know how Julie had contrived to send me a holiday snapshot which included Klemper.

'It's an encouraging sign.'

Pawson was talking about the incident at my flat.

'I'm glad you think so,' I said, fingering the plaster on my neck. 'If my head had been blown off I suppose you would have called it an outstanding success.'

'Hardly.' The half smile on Pawson's lips could have

been at the thought of a headless Philis or he could have
been thinking of something quite different. 'I think you'll
agree that the attack proves you've rattled Schnellinger.'

'Of course Schnellinger hasn't rattled me at all,' I put in
quickly. 'I just love people loosing off machine pistols in
my direction.'

My hand once more found its way to the back of my
neck. This was the second bullet wound I'd collected and
I'd decided I didn't want any more.

'In any case,' I added, 'it might have been the Americans.'

Pawson shook his head.

'You're developing a persecution mania. The Americans
wouldn't shed any tears over you, but they've no intention
of becoming directly involved. They started the myth
that Schnellinger wasn't under their direct control when
they allowed him to pick up Brookes. Now we're playing
them at their own game.'

'I suppose that's why SR (two) drew the assignment,' I
said innocently, the opportunity for the gibe too good to
miss. 'It was too delicate a situation to send in the front-
line troops.'

Pawson did his best to ignore the remark. The implication that SR(2) was a minor-league outfit was accurate
enough, but he didn't like to be reminded of the fact. His
latent megalomania made him lust after the power and
resources of one of the top-notch intelligence units.

'Schnellinger must think you persuaded Richter to talk,'
Pawson said, changing the subject. 'If that's the case you've
made a mistake playing dead.'

'You mean I should act as decoy?'

'Exactly.' Pawson seemed pleased with my apparent

calm. 'Once he knows you're alive he'll have another try. Providing you're well covered we should be able to snatch whoever's detailed for the job.'

'Not a chance,' I told him. 'In the first place I'd probably end up dead and I'm not anywhere near that keen on catching up with Schnellinger. In the second place, it isn't necessary. I know where to find Klemper.'

It wasn't easy to surprise Pawson but this time I succeeded. Earlier in the afternoon I'd told him we were up against a brick wall, now I was telling him I knew where to locate Schnellinger's second-in-command. He wasn't to know I had friends who could write.

'Take a look at this,' I said, handing him the photograph. 'Not at the girl in the bikini but the man standing behind her.'

Pawson studied the photograph carefully, holding it up to the light.

'It's Klemper all right,' he confirmed. 'Where was the photo taken?'

'In San Antonio Abad about a week ago. I want to get to Ibiza as fast as you can arrange it, remembering I'm a dead man.'

Pawson nodded.

'Do you want anyone with you?'

'No, not for the moment. Have some men standing by, but for the time being it's more important to find out whether he's still on the island. What you can do is send the photograph down to Records to see what they can dig up about the girl. For what it's worth, she's using the name Julie Aston.'

Pawson's hand was already on the phone before I'd finished speaking.

Ibiza, Spain, February 1972

Maria Miteck, alias Julie Aston, laughed and put her arms around the man's neck, lips parted provocatively. José was very sure of himself by now and did no more than rest his mouth on hers, not kissing her, waiting to be coaxed. Cocky sod, Maria thought, pulling him closer. There was an immediate response, José turning so that the whole front of his body was touching hers, crushing her to him, one hand entangled in her hair as they kissed, his tongue exploring her mouth. Deliberately Maria moved against him, adding fuel to his mounting desire, and the Spaniard abandoned all pretense of being the controlled, masterful lover. Technique gave way to rampant lust and his fingers tugged at the button of her shirt, hands moving inside to squeeze and knead her breasts. Despite herself Maria found the excitement communicating itself to her, her whole body prickling, experiencing little frissons of pleasure at his touch. She pulled his head down to her bosom, holding him tightly.

'Not here, José,' she whispered, her voice shaky. 'Not in the car.'

Slowly José raised his head, trying to distinguish her face in the darkness.

'There's a rug in the trunk,' he said, misunderstanding her.

'No,' Maria answered softly, shaking her head. 'I'm not that cheap. I only perform in bed.'

On the point of saying it was impossible, José changed his mind, aware of the hand at the top of his thigh, caressing him persuasively. Nestor at the gate would be no problem, Hans should be with the prisoner, so, provided

Maria left early enough, there was no reason why Klemper should ever know she'd been there.

'All right,' he told Maria. 'I'll take you to the villa.'

10

IT WASN'T UNTIL VALENCIA that I realized I was being followed, and even then I found it hard to believe. For a start
I was supposed to be dead, machine-gunned into an early
grave, and not many people were likely to waste time and
money in keeping tabs on a certified corpse. As if this
wasn't enough, no one could possibly have seen me leave
SR(2) headquarters. Pawson and I had considered the
possibility of there being the odd skeptic or two among the
opposition, the kind of people who wouldn't accept I was
really dead until they'd placed a couple of pennies over my
eyes, and our plans had been made accordingly. In the
space of two hours nine different vehicles had left the
underground car park, three of them closed vans, and I'd
departed in the tenth, in the trunk of Pawson's Humber
with the spare tire and a nasty smell of petrol to keep me
company. Uncomfortable and stuffy as the trunk was, I'd
gone the whole hog, all the way to Pawson's house in Rich-
mond, not moving from my hiding place until the garage
doors were closed behind the car.

Up to this point there had been odds of at least a hundred to one against anyone still being in contact. After this
they just hadn't had a chance. The only ways into the
extensive garden at the rear were via the house itself,
through a gate at the side of the house, which was kept

locked, or through the second door to the garage. I'd gone from the garage, vaulted over the wall at the bottom of the garden without bumping into any fairies, and followed the path beside the river for a quarter of a mile, walking to where Soames was waiting. From there, after some more dodging around for my own peace of mind, we'd made for Gatwick where I'd joined the half-full One-Eleven on a package flight to Alicante. With all these precautions it did nothing for my morale to sense I was being tailed. Either it was someone very clever or very lucky and, whichever it was, he was definitely dangerous.

While ESP certainly wasn't one of my pet beliefs, neither was it something I'd dismiss out of hand. I'd left the Astoria Palace painfully short on sleep, heading for the harbor where I hoped to meet a man called George Martin, and knew I'd picked up a tail within fifty yards. The streets were crowded, there was no one breathing heavily down my neck, but there was no doubt at all in my mind. Far too many people confused instinct with being fanciful and, in my profession, they were the men who lived in coffins. My ambition to outlast Methuselah depended on a lot of factors for fulfillment, and absolute faith in my instincts was one of the most important. Therefore, although there was nothing to substantiate my conviction, I began to behave like someone who knew he was being followed. All thoughts of meeting George Martin temporarily shelved, I angled off into a maze of side streets, not so much intent on losing my tail as on finding a nice, quiet bar. A spot of careful thinking was called for and alcohol had always helped to stimulate my brain.

*

The bar I selected was genuine Spanish, not the sort the average tourist included in his itinerary. There was sawdust on the floor, the urinal was only partly concealed by a skimpy bead curtain which did nothing to ease the foul smell, and there were the odd million or so flies buzzing around the hams hung on one wall. To compensate for this, the brandy was good, the prices were Spanish and there were very few customers. By my second drink I still hadn't worked out how I'd managed to collect an entourage, but I would have bet a year's salary on the fact that I had. This was mainly because John Sutters had just come into the bar.

'You'll end up as an alcoholic,' he said as he eased himself into a chair.

If possible he looked even more tired than I felt.

'I've already developed the amnesia,' I told him. 'I seem to have lost a fortnight of my life in East Berlin.'

It wasn't difficult to tell how badly Sutters felt about the double-cross. Even when he'd stopped laughing a smile remained.

'I have to admit that it was my idea, Philis,' he said, without the semblance of a blush. 'It was something I owed you after London.'

Although the explanation might be satisfactory from his point of view, it wasn't from mine. Since East Berlin the agreement with the Russians had been stone dead, and there was only one reason why Sutters should be keen on joining forces with me again. Despite the two weeks' head start he'd gained, he'd been unable to turn up anything useful. Now he was hoping to reach Schnellinger on my coattails. Although this wasn't the way I saw the situation developing, the bar was far too public for me to tell Sutters there.

An indication of Sutters's confidence was that he'd booked in at the Astoria Palace, the same hotel as I, and we established temporary headquarters in his room. How temporary was something only I knew.

'How did you manage to follow me here?' I asked as a start.

Once my curiosity was satisfied it would be the finish as well.

'It was easy.' Sutters grinned. 'You were under surveillance from the moment you landed at Heathrow. One of our men was on hand during the fireworks display at your flat. He thought you'd been killed.'

'A reasonable enough assumption,' I commented, remembering the stream of bullets pouring in through the window.

'I didn't think so,' Sutters told me, widening his smile. 'I couldn't think why Schnellinger should take the risk of having you killed, not unless he thought you knew something. In that case he should have had a go at me as well, but during my fortnight at large he made no attempt on my life.'

Sutters paused, allowing me time to appreciate the argument. I had to admit it made some sense, even if Sutters was completely wrong.

'Then I considered the possibility of you actually having a lead I knew nothing about,' he continued, 'and the shooting seemed more reasonable. It began to look like something Pawson had cooked up to allow you to drop out of circulation. That was when I flew to Paris and arranged for a watch to be kept at all the airports in the London area, a long shot but it came off. As soon as I heard you'd boarded a plane to Alicante I chartered transport to follow you. That's all there was to it.'

'Very clever,' I said, less than impressed.

My initial assessment of the tail had been spot on. Sutters was certainly dangerous and so lucky he could probably fall into a cesspool and discover oil. He'd started with a series of misconceptions and misinterpretations and somehow come up with the right answer. He was overdue for the piece of bad luck I had on ice for him.

'Now I've explained the workings of my brilliant mind perhaps you'd like to tell me why we're in Valencia,' Sutters suggested.

'John, old friend,' I said sadly, 'I'm afraid I don't like. In fact, unless you lie facedown on the bed with your hands behind your head you're well on the way to losing an arm or a leg.'

Sutters looked at the gun I was holding, just to make sure it was really pointing at him, but made no move to obey. He didn't seem particularly surprised and he wasn't at all frightened.

'You wouldn't shoot me, Philis,' he told me, trying to convince me.

'Wrong again,' I said. 'I don't want to hurt you but if I have to I will. Since you left me with Raskin I've decided I prefer to work alone.'

After a second's hesitation Sutters arranged himself on the bed, something of a relief. It was bad enough killing people I didn't like without starting on my friends.

The *Vigo* was a size larger than the other fishing boats in the harbor, its curiously un-Mediterranean lines making it seem out of place. Built of wood, it had originally been a shrimping boat based on the Wash, but when George Martin had taken over there had been some alterations. Apart from moving the vessel's home port to Valencia, he'd installed a new engine which gave a surprising turn of speed for a boat of such unwieldy design, and he'd also stopped trying to reap the harvest of the sea. Instead he'd concentrated on the more profitable business of smuggling, anything from cigarettes to guns.

There was no one on deck, so I dumped my suitcase and clambered down the wide wooden steps into the dark of the main cabin. All the bunks were empty and Martin was the only person there, sitting at a table playing solitaire and doing his best to resemble a smuggler. Starting at the top and working down, there was a battered yachting cap, blue eyes separated by a hooked nose, a dark beard, white teeth to contrast nicely with his bronzed skin, a navy blue T-shirt with short sleeves to display his tattoos, greasy white trousers and a pair of rope sandals on his unstockinged feet. He was the right size for the part as well, about my height with an impressive breadth of chest, and he even had a well-chewed, unlit cheroot between his teeth. While I absorbed the salient details, he showed his interest in his unexpected guest by continuing to play solitaire.

'I'm a friend of Peter Collins',' I said to break the ice.

'Is that meant to be a recommendation?'

He said this without removing the cheroot or turning his head from the cards. So far he gave every indication of being someone who always wore an UP YOURS badge on his shirt.

'I suppose not,' I admitted, deciding I liked him.

He continued playing cards and I leant against what I took to be a bulwark, smoking a cigarette. The game didn't come out and Martin consoled himself by draining the last half liter or so from the bottle of wine he had on hand, disdaining the help of a glass.

'I've seen it all before,' I told him. 'Can we cut the act and talk business?'

For the first time Martin turned toward me, apparently amused.

'I spend hours practicing in front of the mirror,' he said. 'I'd hate the effort to be wasted.'

'Don't worry,' I assured him. 'I'll nominate you for an Oscar.'

'You're a sarcastic sod.' Martin grinned. 'The price of a trip to San Antonio has just gone up.'

Martin had intended to catch me off balance and he succeeded. For a minute or so I rested my chin on my knees, endeavoring to regain my composure.

'You'd make a lousy poker player,' Martin said cheerfully, watching me push my jaw back into place.

'Don't think I'm the inquisitive type,' I managed, 'but how the hell did you know I want to go to San Antonio? I don't remember sending out a printed itinerary.'

'An educated guess,' he lied in a tone of voice which indicated he'd told me everything he intended to. 'How do you want to pay? Pesetas, dollars or sterling?'

'Sterling,' I answered absently, still perplexed by the quality of his guesswork.

'Fair enough. The trip will cost you two hundred fifty pounds and the same again if we run into trouble.'

This time I kept my mouth closed but shot my eyebrows up into my hairline. Although £250 was an awful lot of money to pay for covering sixty-odd miles by sea, it was the calm way Martin accepted the possibility of trouble which had me worried. He was in possession of some information I didn't have and I suspected this was a gap in my education I'd live to regret.

'You're expecting trouble?' I inquired as casually as possible.

'Let's just say I'm an optimist,' Martin replied as he walked toward the companionway.

It was after midnight when I was disturbed by someone roughly shaking my shoulder. My awakener was a Tunisian, one of the three members of Martin's crew, and a man who looked as if he would have made his living by slitting throats in quiet back streets if he hadn't become a sailor. Probably he kept it up as a hobby.

'George wants to see you in the wheel house,' he said in Spanish.

Half-asleep, I tumbled out of the bunk and pulled on the thick sweater Martin had lent me. I'd always thought of Spain as a warm country, and Valencia had been, but it seemed there was a winter at sea just the same as everywhere else. Up on deck there was a slight breeze, the sea running at no more than a gentle swell. Even so, landlubber that I was, I had to scuttle from handhold to handhold while the Tunisian rushed ahead like a frisky mountain goat. Martin was leaning against one of the glass walls of the wheelhouse, munching an outsize sandwich and looking over the shoulder of one of the Spanish members of the crew, who was doing the driving.

'Where are we?' I asked once I'd found something to prop me up.

'We're nearly there. That's the island of Conejera.' Martin indicated a light two or three miles ahead and off the port bow. Or starboard as the case may be. All I knew was that it was to my right. 'The lighthouse is just outside San Antonio Bay.'

Nodding wisely, I cast a knowledgeable, nautical eye over the rest of the seascape. This was mainly sea and darkness apart from the navigation lights of a ship less than a mile away.

'There's another ship,' I commented intelligently.

'It's the reason I called you up on deck,' Martin answered. 'What do you make of it?'

A prompt answer would have been nothing. The dim outline suggested an ordinary fishing boat, with just one exception. Somebody on board was flashing a light at us.

'There's someone on deck with a flashlight,' I told Martin. 'Either the light has a duff battery or it's a signal.'

'He's flashing us a distress signal.' Martin was sneering at me in a complacent manner. 'I don't believe he's in trouble at all.'

'You don't?'

Once again I had the feeling Martin possessed some information I ought to be sharing. This made me uncomfortable.

'No. I think whoever is on board wants to check my cargo.' His smile widened fractionally. 'In fact I think he wants to know whether I'm transporting anybody to San Antonio. The sort of person Peter Collins might have as a friend.'

Casually I adjusted my position. When I'd finished my gun was aimed at Martin's navel.

'There's just been a mutiny, Captain,' I announced, risking a quick glance round to see where the Tunisian was. 'You owe me an explanation.'

Martin was so scared he didn't dare to shake. After he'd lit his cheroot he flashed his teeth at me, a friendly, condescending smile.

'Put your gun away and you shall have it.'

Obediently I did as he'd suggested, belatedly realizing that the gun had been a mistake. If Martin had had fell designs upon my person he'd already had hundreds of opportunities to dispose of me without calling me to the wheel house for a game of cat and mouse.

'I'm all ears,' I said.

It wasn't much of a remark but it was better than asking him to fill me in. Either way he would have laughed.

'Last night,' Martin began, 'before I even knew you existed, I was talking to a friend of mine, Paul Hawkins. He's an American and in the same line of business. He mentioned he'd landed a new job, checking up on all craft going into San Antonio harbor. I didn't think a great deal about it at the time — it wasn't my affair — but when you turned up the connection was obvious. I haven't mentioned this before because I couldn't be sure Paul would be on duty; now I am.' He paused for effect. 'The distress signal is coming from his ship.'

My nod of acknowledgment was rather absent-minded. Bumping into Sutters in Valencia had been bad enough without finding a patrol boat lying in wait. Either Pawson was serializing my progress in a daily newspaper or somebody had a bloody good soothsayer.

'How long has your friend been doing this?' I asked, although I had a fair idea of the answer.

'Tonight is his début.'

Martin was imperturbable as ever. Shuttling smuggled goods backward and forward across the Mediterranean, he was probably accustomed to being stopped, whether by coast guards or hijackers.

'What do you want to do?' he inquired. 'We can take them out for that extra two hundred fifty pounds.'

'What with?'

He had me off balance again.

'I believe in catering for emergencies,' Martin said modestly. 'There's a rifle and a couple of Stirlings aboard.'

It was some emergency he was prepared for. With that firepower Martin could take on most of the Spanish navy.

At the beginning of February the water in the Mediterranean might be blue, but it was also freezing cold and after five minutes in the briny I knew why I'd never joined the rush for a New Year's dip in the Serpentine. Teeth chattering, puckered skin turning blue, I clung to the end of the rope and wished I'd been able to accept the offer to blow Hawkins's fishing boat out of the water. Although this wouldn't have been overdifficult, such an action would have advertised my arrival in Ibiza as surely as if I'd been seen. I'd mentioned this to Martin, together with a reminder that once we'd opened fire with the Stirlings Hawkins could no longer be classified as one of his friends.

'O.K.,' Martin had agreed. 'We'll play it straight.'

'I think so, provided you've a good enough reason for being on the way to San Antonio.'

'That's no problem. I'm ferrying across a consignment of Ducados.'

'Ducados? They're Spanish cigarettes, aren't they?'

Martin had grinned.

'Some antisocial character knocked off a truckload last weekend. I'm taking them to a friend of mine on the island. There's always a shortage in the tourist season.'

His reasons for shipping the cigarettes hadn't interested me in the slightest, only the fact that he had cover for the trip, something which meant he could allow Hawkins and company on board for a quiet look round. There had to be somewhere I could hide for the duration and I'd suggested this to Martin.

'Not a chance,' he'd said, shaking his head. 'Hawkins is in the game too. He knows every place on the *Vigo* large enough to conceal a passenger.'

'What's the alternative?'

'It looks like bath night.' Martin had been really cheerful. 'You have a few tots of whisky, then go over the side.'

At the time the idea hadn't bothered me at all as I hadn't realized the water of the Mediterranean would be cold enough for icebergs. While Martin had been answering the flashed signals from the other boat and moving in closer, I had taken his advice about the whisky, delaying going overboard until the two vessels were less than a hundred yards apart. Only then had I started to wish I were a polar bear.

Wrapped in a couple of blankets, a tumbler of whisky clutched firmly in one hand, I sat in the cabin and shivered quietly. By the clock I'd been in the water a mere thirty-five minutes but it had seemed more like thirty-five hours.

'They were looking for you all right,' Martin remarked.

'I gathered that when they rowed all round the ship,' I mumbled. 'I had a marvelous time swimming backward and forward under the keel.'

Although I didn't mention it I'd been frightened as well. Having a swim from a beach was one thing, doing it with about ten miles of water beneath me was another.

'What excuse did Hawkins make for the distress signal?' I asked.

I wasn't particularly interested but my teeth didn't chatter so much when I was talking.

'He didn't bother,' Martin answered. 'Hawkins came aboard with two heavies and asked if they could have a scout round. They looked in all the obvious places, had a drink, then cleared off. I think they were only going through the motions. Since Hawkins had told me all about his new job, the last thing he'd expect me to do would be to take a passenger straight into San Antonio. He'd reason that if I did try to slip you in I'd use some quiet beach.'

'That's just what I want you to do,' I said. 'There might be somebody keeping an eye on the harbor.'

'You're the boss. Tell me where you want to go and you're as good as there.'

The Tunisian and another member of the crew left me ashore near Cala Bassa, putting in some good, healthy exercise with the oars of the dinghy. It was still dark, only half-past three in the morning, and the rocks did nothing to make life enjoyable. The pleasure boats from San Antonio all possessed gangplank affairs to help tourists ashore, but the *Vigo*'s skiff boasted no such amenities, and it was a tricky business jumping onto the rocks, with suitcase in hand and only a rough idea of where I was going to land. I managed this safely, however, much to the disappointment of the two men in the boat who were both hoping I'd fall back into the sea or break a leg to compensate for their long row, and began working myself through the rocks into the belt of pine trees.

Twenty minutes later I struck the road, or track, leading into town, high time for a rest. Although there was nothing I would have liked better than to find a warm bed, I couldn't afford to head directly for San Antonio. Arriving in the small hours with my suitcase in the middle of the slack season, I would have stuck out like a sore thumb, so stoically I settled down under a tree to wait for dawn. By seven in the morning I was suffering from every known form of exposure except indecent, my blood not starting to circulate properly until I'd done ten minutes' hard walking. After this, with the sky lightening every second, it wasn't so bad, and I reached Port del Torrent in good time. A taxi was waiting for me there, sent by Martin, which made the rest of the trip into San Antonio a lot easier on my feet.

Julie's letter had informed me she was staying at the Hotel Royal, one of the big, new hotels on the Punta Muli, but I had the taxi drive me straight past. It was still early morning, not yet half-past eight, and I needed to establish a base. With this in mind I disembarked in the Calle San Vicente, then cut through the side streets to a small building on the Calle San Antonio which had been converted into three flats. The flat I was interested in was on the first floor, the property of one Arthur Stackpole, a London accountant. For the duration of my stay in Ibiza I was to regard myself as his guest, to use the flat as if it were my own. Mr. Stackpole knew nothing about this, of course, but both Pawson and I had been convinced he'd be only too glad for the place to have a proper airing. A generous guest, I even managed to let myself in without ruining the lock.

The forty winks I'd intended to enjoy stretched to nearly four hours, meaning it was lunchtime before I reached the Royal. My intention had been to treat Julie to a meal, this idea coming to nothing when I found her room key on its hook and failed to locate her in either the restaurant or bar. Rather than sit out the afternoon in the hotel, I hailed my third taxi of the day and returned to the town center.

While I chomped away busily at an indifferent paella, my brain was as active as my teeth. I'd been prepared to accept Sutters's presence in Valencia at face value as the result of an unholy streak of luck, but the patrol boat outside the harbor couldn't be dismissed so easily. It seemed someone had been expecting my arrival in Ibiza and, considering that less than forty-eight hours before I myself hadn't known I was coming, I had to understand the how and why. However often I assembled and correlated the available data only two possible explanations emerged. By far the most likely was that I'd deliberately been led into a trap, that Julie's letter had been specifically designed to lead me to an execution in Ibiza, but this assumption made the machine-gunning of my flat more of a mystery than it was already. Another point this theory failed to explain was how Julie had contrived to meet me in the first place. On the other hand, my second hypothesis was so unlikely it might even be correct. Either way enlightenment would not come until I had contacted Julie.

'Hotel Royal.'

The voice of the desk clerk sounded bored. He was probably on a strict diet, building up his strength to deal with the hordes of young female tourists in the summer.

'I'd like to speak to one of your guests,' I told him. 'A Miss Aston.'

'She's out at the moment,' he answered, the speed of his reply indicating he wasn't in complete hibernation. 'Would you like to leave a message?'

'I'd better,' I said. 'Tell Miss Aston I'll phone again in an hour. The name is Philis.'

There was no harm in the desk clerk knowing my name. As far as I could see I was destined to become one of the island's major tourist attractions.

The Tom and Jerry bar wasn't everybody's cup of tea, but I wasn't particularly interested in tea and, to my mind, it was as good a place to drink Fundador as any. Better, in fact, because it was a small, narrow bar, largely concealed from the street. Most passers-by wouldn't notice the bar was there, and those who did were unlikely to be tempted inside, probably preferring to patronize one of the bigger, brasher bars. All this made it ideal for passing an undisturbed hour, the only other customers being locals, and I managed three drinks before I phoned Julie again. This time she was there.

'Philis,' she exclaimed breathlessly. 'What on earth are you doing in San Antonio?'

Even over a Spanish telephone the youthful ingenuousness came through. Perhaps she really didn't know the answer to her own question. Perhaps the photograph including Klemper really had been a coincidence. Perhaps I'd go mad and take her at face value.

'I came to see you,' I told her. 'It was lonely in the flat without a down-and-out to share my bed.'

'Really?'

This was another exclamation of delighted surprise, suggesting she hadn't realized I'd come hotfoot to Ibiza as soon as I received her letter.

'Really,' I assured her. 'How soon can you be ready to give me a guided tour of the island?'

There was a brief silence while she considered the knotty problem. A cynic might have suspected she was calculating how long it would take her to arrange a reception committee.

'You'd better give me an hour,' she decided. 'I'll have to shower and change.'

'That's fine,' I answered amenably. 'I'll meet you in the bar.'

San Antonio Abad, Spain, February 1972

Ramirez lay on the hotel bed, cigarette clamped between his lips, eyes screwed up against the smoke as he scrutinized the photograph he held in his left hand. It was a portrait, in color, depicting the head and shoulders of a man in his early thirties. The face was unmistakably English, Ramirez decided, despite the dark hair and the heavily tanned skin, and the good-natured smile wasn't to be trusted. It was the eyes which gave him away, watchful and cold, unrelaxingly vigilant even when faced by a harmless camera. He was a fellow pro, someone who knew what it was like to kill, and Ramirez hoped he managed to reach Ibiza. Dead, the Englishman was worth $10,000, but before he died he might provide some entertainment.

Discarding the photograph, Ramirez rolled off the bed and crossed the room to stand in front of the mirror above the washbasin, cigarette drooping from the corner of his mouth. His reflection stared back at him, an arrogant, aristocratic face, the touch of gray at his temples and the prominent, beaked nose giving his features a distinguished air, the mustache doing something to disguise the cruel lines of his thin-lipped mouth. Ramirez still stood in front of the mirror, completely satisfied with what he saw, when there was a tap at the door.

'Come in,' he called without turning his head.

'He's here,' the newcomer announced, slightly out of breath.

'You're sure?'

'Yes.' The man's tone was positive. 'I saw him myself.'

Slowly Ramirez smiled into the mirror, congratulating himself on his good fortune, then bent his head to look at his watch. There was plenty of time for him to earn his money before dinner.

11

Rather than proceed directly to the Hotel Royal, a journey of less than ten minutes, I preferred to have another couple of drinks in the Tom and Jerry, filling in time until Julie had finished titivating herself or whatever. I found the darkened interior of the bar very soothing, especially as there were no foreigners in evidence. Spaniards I was prepared to trust, anyone with a different foreign accent made me nervous, which all went to prove how wrong I could be.

'Do you mind if I join you, Señor Philis?' the Spaniard asked politely.

Actually there were plenty of things I minded — his use of my name, the familiar manner in which he was leaning against me and, most of all, the hard object he was pressing into the back of my neck. The light material of the jacket didn't fool my tactile sense at all and I was finding the occurrence almost monotonous. Wherever I went, Nottingham, Berlin or Ibiza, the first major happening was that somebody waved a gun in my direction.

'For God's sake,' I said. 'Why can't you have the decency to leave me alone?'

The Spaniard laughed confidently before seating himself beside me. He also looked confident, probably because a second man had sat down on my other side and there was a third ordering drinks at the bar. Worse still, he exuded an air of competence, behaving as though menacing me with a gun was part and parcel of his everyday business, routine and nothing more. The prospect of offensive action by me didn't worry him at all. He was certain he had a counter for any move I chose to make and he convinced me as well. The man was a professional killer, a modern-day bounty hunter. I knew because I occasionally had to look in the mirror myself.

'Do we have any introductions?' I asked after the third man had joined us, my mouth unpleasantly dry.

I addressed my query to the Spaniard, the one I was already thinking of with a capital S. His companions were fellow countrymen but of no great importance, just extra guns. The Spaniard shook his head in reply to my question.

'Salud,' he said, raising his glass.

'Cheers,' I replied, dreaming up an original answer.

My glass went up in my left hand, one knee was brushing the underside of the table and my free hand was six inches away from the butt of my gun in its shoulder holster. The idea was born of desperation, one of the long shots which comprised my full armory, and it was almost a relief when the Spaniard stamped painfully on my instep.

'I just saved your life,' he remarked conversationally as I relaxed. 'Hold the glass in your other hand.'

This was when I realized I was going to die. If, in a similar situation, anyone else had knowingly left me armed, I would have thought he was taking a completely unwarranted risk, doing his best to have himself shot. With the Spaniard this yardstick didn't apply. He knew exactly what he was doing, considering the gun in my possession less dangerous than an attempt to disarm me in public.

Surprisingly the realization had a tranquilizing effect, enabling me to assess my position logically, unhampered by any traces of optimistic euphoria. The Spaniard would make no mistakes, had no intention of being caught off guard, so there was no sense in building castles in the air. My only choice seemed to lie in how I chose to be killed — running, fighting or standing still.

'Are you ready?' the Spaniard inquired.

He'd emptied his glass and was obviously keen to go. Although I wasn't nearly as enthusiastic, I didn't have much say in the matter.

'What for?' I asked, meeting his question with another, intent on adding precious seconds to my existence.

'We're going for a ride in the country.'

There was the slightest shadow of a smile on his lips. He had a fair idea of what was going on in my mind.

'I'd hate to upset your plans,' I said tentatively, 'but let's suppose, just for argument's sake, that I don't fancy a drive.'

'It's entirely up to you.' The Spaniard was mocking me now. 'If you want a few innocent bystanders injured stay here by all means.'

The sudden spurt of hatred was so intense it was a wonder it didn't burn my eyeballs to a frazzle. The fact that the Spaniard intended to kill me was something I had to accept, however unwillingly — this was his job. His evident amusement was a different matter altogether, for, in my humble opinion, nobody's death was a laughing matter, least of all mine. The Spaniard was playing with me, hoping to provoke me either into resistance or flight because the simple act of killing me was far too easy. His attitude derived from a motive beyond straightforward sadism.

Human life was irrelevant compared with his own enjoyment.

'Where's the car?' I asked tightly, my voice shaking slightly.

His two companions undoubtedly thought this was the product of fear but not the Spaniard. He knew I wouldn't die easily and the knowledge pleased him.

The car, a Seat 600, was parked at the bottom of the Calle Ramon y Cajal and the walk offered me plenty of opportunities to commit suicide. At every step I was conscious of the weight of the gun against my left side, positive I wouldn't be allowed to retain it for much longer. Even with the Spaniard walking on my left, the other two directly behind, this should have been the time to attempt a break, while I was still armed, but the streets remained obstinately full of pedestrians, people who had as fervent a desire to live as I had.

'The town is busy for this time of year,' the Spaniard commented cheerfully, accurately interpreting my thoughts.

'Isn't it?' I grunted.

At the car the street was temporarily clear, not that this did me any good. One of the Spaniard's acolytes clambered in first, I entered next and the Spaniard completed the sandwich in the back seat, the third man acting as chauffeur. For every second I was under the direct threat of at least two guns.

With everybody safely aboard we took the Avenida Doctor Fleming, the line of hotels to our right, and drove in the direction of San José. Once San Antonio was behind us the Spaniard decided I had no further need of my gun, or anything else come to that, even taking my cigarettes. I could appreciate his point, realizing the average corpse had no great need for a smoke.

'Are we going to see Klemper?' I asked, as the buildings of San José came into view.

'Who's Klemper?' Ramirez quipped. I'd learnt his name by listening to my captors' desultory conversation.

In San José we turned left onto the road swinging round toward the city of Ibiza, but this was hardly likely to be our destination. If so we would have followed the Carretera Ibiza from San Antonio. In any case, the largest town on the island wasn't the place to stage an execution. The rocky, scrub-covered hills to the left seemed a far better location and my guess was confirmed when we left the main road, climbing a narrow, spring-wrecking track. After ten minutes' bouncing and bumping we stopped.

'This is the end of the line,' Ramirez informed me.

He had a great ear for an original phrase.

For the whole way from the Ibiza road the track had hugged closely to the hillside, uneven and barely wide enough for one car, but where we'd halted, just past one of the innumerable corners, there was approximately half an acre of level ground. As Ramirez had said, this was literally the end of the line, the track petering out completely, its terminal a long since abandoned stone hut. The spot was almost ideal for would-be murderers, isolated and enclosed, the surrounding hills making it a miniature amphitheater. To one side of the bowl there was a ravine some thirty yards across, heavily studded with rocks and small trees at the bottom, the cover they offered as inaccessible as the mountains of the moon.

Ever since Ramirez had appeared in the Tom and Jerry

bar I'd known what was in store for me; now its inevitability really struck home, and although my limbs didn't turn to jelly they did feel as if they might cave in at the joints. There was no great delay before I had the opportunity to prove the sensation was largely illusory.

Procedure for ushering me out of the Seat was every bit as competent as the performance in San Antonio, and I was beginning to find my captors' professionalism rather depressing. I hadn't expected them to make any silly blunders, but apparently I'd been wrong in my assessment of Ramirez, the one faint glimmer of hope I'd had to spur me on. I'd placed him as somebody who had killed so often that the process had become boring and mechanical, that to get his kicks he had to needle me into resistance or an attempt to break free. Now I wasn't quite so sure. For me to fight or run the odds against success had to be down in the low thousands, a mark which hadn't yet been approached.

The derelict hut played no part in Ramirez's plans. Instead he made for a flat rock in the center of the bowl, where he seated himself, his henchmen arrayed one on either side of him. With a peremptory wave of his gun he waved me to a spot some ten yards away, my back to the ravine and too far away from him for me to have any clever ideas. Satisfied I was correctly positioned, Ramirez pocketed his gun and lit a cigarette. The other two still had weapons in evidence but they didn't matter. From the beginning I'd had the feeling that the issue lay between Ramirez and myself.

'You know why we're here?' Ramirez asked.

'For some yodeling practice?' I suggested.

My heart wasn't in it and I failed to amuse myself.

Ramirez was amused, however. He discerned I was likely to wet my pants at any second.

'Hardly,' he said. 'I've been instructed to kill you.'

He paused to allow me an opportunity to absorb the information, something of a waste of time. Being a bright boy, I'd guessed this from the start.

'However,' Ramirez continued, 'I've decided to exceed my instructions.'

'Naughty.'

My stock of infantile chatter should last for hours.

'I thought it might prove interesting to learn whom you telephoned shortly before I introduced myself. Checking at the post office would be a tedious process and I'm sure my employer will be delighted to know who your contact is on the island.' He took an appreciative pull at his cigarette. 'Do you want to tell me?'

'I'm sorry,' I said. 'It's classified information.'

'I thought that might be your attitude,' Ramirez remarked calmly. 'In fact, I very much doubt whether I can persuade you to talk.'

This was accompanied by a friendly smile. Although he was probably complimenting me, I couldn't muster a smile in reply.

'Nevertheless, I'm prepared to try,' he continued. 'We have plenty of time.' Another drag at his cigarette. 'In five minutes I intend to shoot you in the right knee. Half an hour after that, if you still refuse to cooperate, I shall treat your left knee in the same fashion. Half an hour later it will be your groin and so on. How does the idea appeal to you?'

Privately I suspected Ramirez had every chance of persuading me to cooperate, but I could hardly tell him so.

'I wouldn't like it at all,' I admitted. 'There must be some other way we can spend the afternoon.'

What I would have liked was a detailed map of the ground behind me. According to my calculations, five steps and a dive should see me over the edge of the ravine, less than a second in time. Whether this would gain me anything apart from a broken neck I didn't know, but Ramirez obviously expected me to try. That was why he'd put away his gun.

'You have four minutes,' Ramirez told me.

Before he'd finished speaking I was pivoting on my left heel, thrusting off from a standing start. Four long strides were all I allowed myself, then I was diving over the lip of the ravine, knowing full well that I wouldn't find any water at the bottom.

Shale was what I found, great quantities of shale, hitting it hard some ten feet below the rim, striking first with my hands and forearms, then with my chin. The next forty feet down the steeply shelving slope were covered in a tangle of mixed-up limbs, as I rolled, bounced and slid until I hit rock bottom. Or, to be more precise, the rock at the bottom. Normally I'd have lain where I was, waiting for a passing ambulance, but I wasn't too battered to ignore the threat from above, forcing myself the few lurching steps to the protection of the nearest jumble of rocks.

'What on earth do you think you're doing, Philis?' Ramirez shouted from the clifftop.

He seemed remarkably unconcerned about the loss of his intended prey. Moreover, there had been only two shots before I dropped out of sight, both of them missing, which meant Ramirez had fired neither of them. There had been no accident about my position close to the edge of the ravine or about the way Ramirez had wasted time in idle conversation. He'd wanted me to reach the comparative safety of the ravine, otherwise I wouldn't have been there. The question was, why?

Two minutes later there was still no sign of hectic activity above, no more than a quiet murmur of voices, and before I attempted to answer the self-imposed query I reviewed my physical condition. Although my initial impression — that every bone in my body had been broken — proved to be false, I wasn't exactly unscathed. Those parts of me which weren't bruised were either grazed or cut, and a couple of ribs felt as if they might be cracked. Otherwise I was fine.

This diagnosis left me free to consider what I'd achieved by diving over a fifty-foot cliff, preliminary observation suggesting I wasn't much better off. Admittedly, there were no men pointing guns at me, but, on the debit side, I could see no ready-made avenue of escape. I had no intention of climbing back to where I'd left Ramirez and friends, the opposite side resembled the north face of the Eiger without the ice, and the end of the ravine, where two hills met, was scalable only if someone lowered me a rope. My sole hope was to follow the bottom of the gully, trusting it led somewhere useful.

Where the track above had bent sharply round the corner of a hill there was a corresponding dogleg in the ravine, some sixty yards from my place of concealment. Cautiously and painfully, using every scrap of cover offered by the rocks and the foliage of the trees, I crawled toward it, keeping close to the cliff I'd descended. My efforts would have won me no prizes in a sprint competition, not unless I had snails for opposition, and I took ten minutes to reach the bend. When I eventually did arrive, and could see round the corner, I discovered why Ramirez hadn't been upset. A hundred yards past the dogleg the miniature valley abruptly ended in a shale slope which completely sealed it off. The slope could be climbed easily enough, but this would take a good five minutes, five minutes when I'd be exposed to the three men above.

Luckily I had a sense of humor and could appreciate how funny my daredevil exploits had appeared. Ramirez must have been crippling himself as he watched me do a swallow dive over the cliff, knowing I was risking a broken neck in order to incarcerate myself in a rock-filled prison some two hundred and fifty yards long by thirty wide. He didn't give a damn about my phone call to Julie — as he said, some-body could check at the exchange — he merely wanted some sport. His idea of what this constituted made fox hunting seem relatively humane.

For the second time that afternoon I was murderously angry, so angry I rose to my feet to see what was happening above. The answer was that everybody was waiting for me to show myself. With bullets richocheting dangerously close I ducked down fast.

'Do you want to surrender?' Ramirez called. 'Or do we have to come down after you?'

There was a nasty-looking piece of jagged rock on the ground beside me and I fancied the thought of what it could do to Ramirez's face. This involved standing up again, to give the Philis right arm full play, and I couldn't have cared less. As a gesture it didn't amount to much — throwing stones at people with guns never did — and my aim was terrible, missing the target by a yard. At least the yelp of pain I heard as I ducked showed I'd hit somebody, which was more than the three above managed.

'Save your strength, Philis,' Ramirez shouted cheerfully. 'We'll be down before dark.'

Of course they would be, and when they came one of them would have his head bashed in. The prospect gave me something to look forward to.

My watch told me the time was nearly three o'clock and I had no reason to accuse it of lying. With any luck, a commodity which had been in short supply recently, I had at least an hour before the manhunt began, possibly an hour and a half. Ramirez wanted me to sweat, to torture myself with fantasies of what might happen, but I intended to put the reprieve to good use. If my position wasn't very healthy, I did have one very small factor in my favor. Although Ramirez had me hopelessly trapped on ground of his choosing, I knew exactly how he planned to kill me, the terrain limiting him almost as much as it did me. Two men would come down, acting as beaters and driving me in front of them until I ran out of ravine. The third man would stay near the top of the shale slope, just in case I somehow managed to break past his companions.

Breaking through the line struck me as far too energetic a pastime, quite apart from being the expected thing to do. On the whole I preferred to allow the two beaters to walk straight past me. The place I selected was near the dogleg, out of sight of anyone guarding the ravine's one and only exit and where one of the larger boulders had an overhang close to the ground. Working with a succession of sharp-edged stones as my only tools, I spent an industrious half an hour, making as little noise as possible and enlarging the hollow until it was big enough for me to crawl in without any stray limbs sticking out. This was a good start and it encouraged me to embark on a series of scavenging expeditions to collect a selection of the larger pieces of loose rock.

This took longer than I'd anticipated, helping me to develop the obsession that Ramirez would come before my preparations were completed. The ravine was a sun trap and I was already sweating profusely, but now I virtually floated away as I frantically concealed evidence of my excavations and sealed myself in the homemade tomb. God only knew what it looked like from outside. From my cramped position it seemed as though a five-year-old playing hide-and-seek could have done better.

As it turned out I needn't have hurried myself, having nearly three quarters of an hour in my pseudo cave to run through every likely permutation of events, exactly what Ramirez wanted me to do. Being shot wasn't what frightened me most, although it certainly wasn't something I was looking forward to. The scene I kept playing to myself came when my rudimentary hiding place was discovered, Ramirez laughing at me as I crouched behind my pitiful rampart of stones. From this humiliation it was all too easy to project the fantasy a stage further, to the point where Ramirez was sealing me in permanently. For a man with my claustrophobic tendencies this image lacked appeal and it was almost a relief when they came for me. As usual Ramirez chose to broadcast his intentions.

'Time's up,' he shouted. 'We're coming down.'

Even so, another quarter of an hour passed before I heard the sounds of their approach, fifteen minutes during which I lost about a gallon of body fluid through my pores.

There were two of them as expected, the Spaniard and one other man, and they made a devil of a lot of noise as they came closer, intentionally, not through carelessness. The sole difference between flushing out a man and a pheasant was that a man might decide to leap from his hiding place with a rock in his hand, more or less what I intended to do, and this was something they'd be prepared for. Although I couldn't see them I was certain they would be taking care to cover each other, ready to provide instant support in the event of an attack. This was why my ambition didn't extend beyond smashing in one head.

Slowly, deliberately, the noise came nearer to where I lay, making it increasingly difficult to continue breathing normally. When someone started coming round the side of the boulder which concealed me I stopped trying to control it, concentrating on cursing myself for not having stayed out in the open, taken my chances like a man instead of a rabbit. Through the chinks in the rocks piled in front of me a pair of blue trousers and light brown shoes came into view, meaning it wasn't Ramirez unless he'd changed his clothes, and I waited tensely for the shout and laughter which would herald discovery. For interminable seconds the man stood no more than a yard away, then he moved on again and my heart dropped down my throat, back into its accustomed place.

For a couple of minutes I remained where I was, partly through discretion, partly to become used to breathing again, then I began to remove the barricade of stones in front of me, being careful to make no noise. Coupled with my caution was an awareness of the need for speed. So far neither of the beaters had caught a glimpse of me and, long before he reached the end of the ravine, Ramirez would guess what I'd done, that I might already be behind him.

Once I'd stretched my cramped limbs I set off after the two men, moving quietly despite the fact they were making as much din as a middling-sized herd of elephants. Apart from being noisy they were also proceeding slowly and I was up with them in no time at all, settling down behind a suitable rock to watch them at work.

A rock-filled stretch of ground some thirty yards wide contained plenty of potential hiding places, and by now Ramirez was probably wishing he'd had an extra man. At their present rate of progress it would take the two of them at least half an hour to reach the end of the gully, mainly because Ramirez had insisted on doing the job thoroughly. He and his companion had split the area in two, Ramirez opting for the left-hand side, the other man the right, both of them taking care not to stray out of visual contact. It was all very neat and orderly — provided they didn't have somebody creeping up on them from the rear, somebody with homicide in his heart.

As I watched them the scope of my ambition increased, widening to include the possibility I might live. No longer did I merely want to bash one or other of them about the head, I wanted to collect a gun as well. Naturally there were an almost infinite number of 'ifs' involved, but, for the first time since I'd met Ramirez, I dared to think of myself as a man with a future. Maybe.

The two hunters moved forward and I went with them, steadily closing up on the man in blue trousers. By now I had their method taped. One of them remained stationary near the center of the gorge while the other investigated a likely-looking cluster of rocks, then the positions were reversed. When Blue Trousers' next turn for sentry duty came, I was a mere two yards from him, a small boulder clutched in my right hand. Any closer and I would have been in the open.

It was difficult to relax as I awaited my opportunity, painfully aware that once I committed myself every scrap of luck available had to drop into my lap, that Blue Trousers had to be dead, his gun in my hand, before Ramirez realized what was happening behind him. This was asking for an awful lot but I very nearly made it. Nearly but not quite.

The man in blue trousers died before he knew he was in any danger. One moment he was keeping a watchful eye on Ramirez's back, the next I had taken two swift, noiseless steps forward and cracked open his skull with the rock, hitting him so hard I must have crumpled every vertebrae in his spine. As he slumped forward my left arm went around his chest to support him, I dropped the rock and grabbed for the gun in his hand. Then the damn fool allowed it to fall from his nerveless fingers.

I was on my knees, my right hand a good foot away from the weapon, when the bullet sprayed soil and splinters of rock into my face. Carefully I wiped the grit from my eyes, leaving my right hand where it was. Ramirez was moving toward me, a slight smile on his lips, eyes bright and feverish, his gun pointing unwaveringly at a point between my eyes. This was the end and I knew it.

Ten feet away from me Ramirez stopped, still smiling and apparently uninterested in the man I'd killed. My whole life didn't flash in front of my eyes, I didn't conjure up nostalgic memories of parents, friends or mistresses, good times or bad. All I could think of was how nice it would be to live to draw an old-age pension.

'Why don't you try for the gun?' Ramirez taunted softly. 'I'm going to shoot you anyway.'

Dully I looked at the automatic, twelve immeasurable inches away from the spread fingers of my right hand.

'It's hardly an even break,' I said.

My voice sounded strange, hoarse and unsteady.

'It's the only one you'll get.'

Futile as it was, we both knew I'd try, the instinct for survival compelling me to, although Ramirez would never allow me to reach the gun. It was either this or run, something which was equally impracticable. I was still nerving myself for the effort when, out of the blue, two shots rang out from the rim of the ravine above us, the bullets whining off the rocks several yards behind Ramirez.

'Jesús!' he bellowed, taken completely by surprise and involuntarily glancing upward.

Not that all this registered consciously at the time. I was aware only of the sharp crack of the shots, the sound jerking me into galvanic motion. Despairingly I snatched at the automatic, beginning to fire as the barrel left the ground. The first two bullets must have hit Ramirez round the kneecaps, the next in the stomach, the rest of the magazine anywhere, holding him spread-eagled against a boulder until I was clicking an empty gun and his corpse could fall to the ground.

The reaction was complete, my trembling so uncontrollable my left arm was unable to support me, and I collapsed face downward, limbs juddering, teeth chattering, my bladder emptying itself unheeded. I might have lain there all night if I hadn't remembered the third man. Still decidedly shaky, I rested my back against a rock while I pieced together the events which had led to my resurrection. Only then did I realize that Ramirez hadn't fired at me, that the two shots had come from above me. Nor had his last utterance been an eleventh-hour conversion, he'd shouted the name of the man he'd left to guard the shale slope. None of this made sense, but it seemed wise to establish contact with my unseen deliverer.

'Jesús,' I shouted. 'Are you there?'

'Why the hell should he be?' a voice replied in English. 'He's got better things to do than look after you.'

At last I did understand. How or why Sutters had arrived on the scene remained a mystery, but he was there and this was enough.

Tel Aviv, Israel, February 1972

The young Palestinian was led out, shoulders slumped, head bowed, the arrogance long since gone. By his own admission the boy was only fourteen, an age when he should have been at school instead of skulking through the streets of a hostile city, a city he'd been told was his rightful home, enough plastic explosive in his possession to kill hundreds of innocent civilians. Although he was momentarily saddened by the thought, not unaware of the parallel to his own youth, Miteck was unable to suppress his high spirits for long and he was whistling under his breath when he reached Brinkmann's office. The General flipped through the synopsis of the interrogation, reading fast but missing nothing.

'Useless,' he said disgustedly once he'd finished, slapping

the report on the desk. 'There's nothing we don't know already. I can't understand why you're looking so smug.'

Miteck smiled cheerfully.

'Maria phoned this afternoon,' he said by way of explanation.

'She's still on holiday, is she?'

'Yes, but she'll be home soon.'

Perplexed, Brinckmann shook his head as Miteck left the room. A bachelor himself, he failed to comprehend why a phone call from a twenty-two-year-old daughter should make a sane, intelligent man walk around with a beatific smile on his lips. He wasn't to know Maria had told her father that Klemper's hours were numbered, that the Englishman, Philis, had at last reached Ibiza.

12

LARGELY BECAUSE MY COORDINATION was shot to pieces, I took closer to twenty minutes to scramble up the shale slope than the five I'd optimistically forecast when I'd still thought I was going to die. Even the cigarette John was smoking couldn't make me move any faster. By the time I reached the top and sank down beside him I was finished, emotionally and physically exhausted. A couple of pygmies could have taken me with all four hands tied behind their backs.

'Your trousers are wet,' John commented sociably.

'I was sweating a lot,' I panted.

I knew damn well that my trousers were soaked, but there'd been no need for him to mention it. His laugh was unnecessary as well.

'They had you worried, did they?'

'Oh no,' I protested. 'All along I knew my fairy god-mother would arrive and turn them into white mice. Now shut up and give me a cigarette.'

Looking superior, John did as I'd suggested, having enough consideration left over to allow me to smoke in peace. Only when I started on the second cigarette did he show any sign of impatience.

'Are you ready to leave yet?' he asked. 'We ought to get back to the road before it's dark.'

'Just wait a second,' I told him. 'I need a change of clothes.'

The body of the man called Jesús was some fifty yards away and the wound in his back had been made by a knife. Considering the nearest cover was forty-five feet distant it was reasonable to assume knife throwing was one of John's specialities.

With a relatively fresh, ill-fitting pair of trousers to make me decent and Jesús' body callously kicked over the edge of the cliff, I was ready to go, agreeing it might be safer if John took the wheel of the Seat. At the first café on the San José road, which looked as though it ought to have a telephone, I told him to stop. Although he must have wondered what I was doing, John didn't raise any objections, or ask any stupid questions. It was tacitly understood that we were operating as a team again, East Berlin and Valencia forgotten.

'Where on earth have you been, Philis?' Julie asked me when she reached the phone. 'I waited nearly two hours for you.'

'I was unavoidably detained,' I explained with what I felt was masterly understatement. 'I'll tell you about it later. What I want you to do, in fact what you're going to do, is pack an overnight bag, go to Jack's Bar and wait for me there.'

'Why . . . ?' Julie began.

Her reaction was so predictable I didn't allow her a chance to get into full stride.

'No questions and forget any prior engagements,' I broke in. 'Just do as I said and I'll see you in an hour.'

With this I put down the receiver, cutting off further protest. John was standing patiently at the bar, drinks set up, and I drank mine in one gulp as I passed through, pushing John in front of me. He didn't protest, but once we were on the road he gave vent to his curiosity.

'Who did you phone?' he inquired. 'The local bookie?'

'The girl who brought me to Ibiza,' I told him, ignoring the feeble humor. 'She knows where Klemper is although she hasn't told me yet. We're taking her off the island with us.'

This kept John quiet for a minute or two. Not the mention of Klemper or the girl but the bit about leaving the island. It was the first he'd heard of such a move.

'Exactly why are we leaving the island?' he asked eventually. 'We've only just arrived.'

'It's part of the keep-Philis-alive campaign. I don't think the three men we disposed of this afternoon were the only people on my trail. Even if they were, Klemper is likely to saturate the area once he realizes they're missing.'

'O.K.,' John agreed after due reflection, 'but it seems rather pointless to travel all the way to the mainland.'

'Who said anything about the mainland? We're going to find out why the hippies were so fond of Formentera.'

We were passing through San José before John finally broke.

'Aren't you going to ask how I was able to come to your rescue?' he said.

'Not likely,' I answered. 'You'll burst a blood vessel soon if you don't tell me how clever you've been. Anyway,' I added, 'I already know.'

'You do?'

Although he didn't actually call me a liar John's tone was distinctly skeptical. He didn't enjoy having his thunder stolen. On the other hand, I welcomed the opportunity to show off. It had taken a lot of hard work to pin-point the mistake I'd made in Valencia, a mistake I was thankful for.

'Of course,' I said casually, giving the impression I'd known all along. 'It was a question of timing. Your man at Gatwick told you I was on a flight to Alicante and you chartered a plane to follow, but you couldn't possibly have touched down before me. Instead you arranged for a local agent to meet me at Alicante airport and he shadowed me to Valencia. When I left you trussed up in the hotel, he must have followed me to the harbor. Once he'd reported back and untied you from the bed, you caught the first flight to Ibiza. From there it was easy. You probably arrived hours before I did.'

'You're covering up, you bastard.' John laughed, his good temper restored. 'You must have been sweating your brains out trying to figure where you'd gone wrong.'

This was a remark I chose to ignore.

Back in San Antonio I directed John along the front to the Hotel Tanit where I told him to park. By now he was becoming accustomed to being treated like a chauffeur.

'Give me your pen,' I said.

John gave it to me with a shrug, watching with interest as I ripped open a packet of Ducados.

'I suppose you know what you're doing.'

'Naturally,' I answered, writing busily.

'That's nice, because I don't. I've already compiled a list of questions the length of my arm.'

'Save them,' I said, handing him his pen and the note. 'You're going for a stroll. The ship you want is the *Vigo*. You can't miss it — it's the biggest and ugliest fishing boat in port. When you get there you find the captain, George

Martin, no one else. Give him the note and tell him you're a friend of mine, then arrange a trip to Formentera. I'll leave you to haggle over the price.'

'What will you be doing?' John asked suspiciously.

'Picking up the girl. It shouldn't take more than half an hour.'

'I'd still like to read the note. For all I know it instructs Martin to kill the bearer on sight.'

John unfolded the packet, then he started laughing.

'God Almighty,' he spluttered. ' "He's like a brother. No swimming this time. Stirling resistance if trouble." Where did you go to school?'

He was still cackling to himself when I booted him out of the car.

Before collecting Julie I had a couple of visits to make. The first was to the post office, where I phoned Pawson, the second was to the apartment I'd appropriated to pick up my suitcase. Arthur Stackpole would never know how little use the accommodation had been to me.

Jack's Bar was only a stone's throw away from the apartment, and Julie was the first person I saw when I drew in to the curb, seated at one of the outside tables. She was looking very demure in a pale blue, sleeveless sweater and white shorts, both garments so tight they would have been underneath her skin if she'd breathed too heavily. As far as I and the other half-dozen males ogling her could see, she still wasn't too taken with the idea of wearing underwear.

'Hurry up,' I called through the car window. 'We haven't got all day.'

Apart from her looks Julie had plenty of other things going for her as well, like a temperament which allowed me to order her around. She didn't even stop to finish her drink, just picked up her blue Air France bag and came to join me in the Seat. Naturally, there were a lot of questions she wanted to ask me but, once she'd noticed the skin I'd scraped from my chin and the long cut down my left cheek, they all boiled down to one.

'What have you been doing to yourself, Philis?' she said by way of greeting, full of maternal concern despite being the junior by over ten years.

'My razor needs a new blade,' I told her, slipping into gear.

Although Julie kept pressing I sidestepped every question she threw at me, far more concerned with leaving San Antonio in one piece. Sooner or later I'd have to offer an explanation, but I preferred later, somewhere I wasn't likely to be shot at any moment. In any case, explanations weren't particularly important. I knew Julie would accompany me wherever I chose to go, something which had nothing to do with my sex appeal.

On board the *Vigo* preparations for a prompt departure were proceeding apace, showing Martin must have screwed John for some exorbitant sum. I'd abandoned the Seat opposite the Florida, more or less where I'd first seen it, and when Julie and I had reached the boat everyone except the Tunisian was down in the cabin. Martin and the other members of his crew were busy stripping down the two submachine guns which formed a substantial part of his armory while John sat on a bunk, looking unhappy.

'The man's a crook,' he said, after an appreciative examination of Julie.

'Of course he is, if you're referring to our worthy captain,' I told him. 'That's why he's prepared to ferry us to Formentera.'

John snorted. Either that or he was suppressing a belch.

'For the price he's charging you'd think he was taking us to New York.'

'You can swim there for all I care,' Martin retorted, eventually managing to tear his eyes away from Julie.

Julie wasn't unaware of the undiluted lust emanating from Martin and Sutters, not to mention the two Spanish deckhands. She'd also noticed the pieces of Stirling littering the cabin.

'Is someone going to tell me what this is all about?' she demanded of me. 'For all I know your friends are mixed up in the white slave traffic.'

For answer I put my hands on her shoulders and kissed her, partly to keep her quiet but mainly because it seemed a hell of a while since I'd last kissed an attractive woman and I'd have hated to get out of practice.

'Now that's an idea,' Martin murmured as he began to reassemble one of the Stirlings.

I assumed he was thinking of Julie's reference to white slavery, wondering whether the *Vigo* was sufficiently sea-worthy to reach Buenos Aires or Beirut.

Not a lot could be said about Formentera because there wasn't a great deal of it to talk about. The southernmost of the Balearics, it was a low-lying, hammer-shaped slab of rock, ringed with lighthouses so that ships didn't sail right over it without noticing the island was there. San Francisco Javier, the chief village, possessed a nice example of an eighteenth-century fortified church if that's what turned you on and, until recently, the island had been an international hippie center if you fancied seeing hippies in the wild. Otherwise the handful of inhabitants fished, made and drank wine and let the hot sun turn sea water into salt. To my mind Formentera's main attraction was that no one would expect me to go there.

We left San Antonio on course for Valencia, going well beyond Hawkins's patrol boat, which was still on duty, unaware of events on Ibiza, before we swung round to the southwest, toward Formentera. Not that I had much to do with this as I was ensconced in Martin's cabin with Julie. Originally the idea had been that she should act as a nautical Florence Nightingale, recruited to take a look at my ribs which had been hurting all afternoon. Stripped to the waist, I lay on Martin's bunk while Julie prodded round and hurt me a lot more, her fingers as gentle as jack-hammers. Eventually she decided nothing was broken, just badly bruised, but insisted I need strapping up with half a mile of bandages. Somehow the nurse-patient relationship broke down about here, and I found Julie on the bunk beside me, sweater discarded on the floor, moaning quietly while I industriously nuzzled her breasts, manipulating my tongue round the taut nipples. She was enjoying herself so much I felt duty bound to help her remove her shorts, persevering with my selfless caresses until she was crying out loud for servicing. It would have been churlish to refuse.

'You'd make a lousy nurse,' I told her afterward, kissing her affectionately while I eased a hand toward my cigarettes.

'Thanks,' she said, cuddling closer.

Although it was probably part of her job she seemed to have appreciated my efforts.

'Don't mention it, Maria. Fulsome flattery is part of my comprehensive service.'

At this she stiffened, suddenly tense. This wasn't because she was afraid I'd drop the lit match on her.

'Aren't you going to complain about the case of mistaken identity?' I asked once the cigarette was lit. 'It's what you're supposed to do.'

Maria raised herself on one elbow to look down at me, all passion gone from her blue eyes. Not that I dwelt on her eyes for long, far preferring the soft curve of the breast swaying above me. It evoked a familiar feeling down below.

'How long have you known?'

'Not very long,' I assured her. 'Only since you sent me the photograph. Even then Records didn't have anything about you except the name Maria Miteck, but they did have quite a lot about your father — he liaised with us during the Suez fiasco. We even know why a Polish Catholic should be working for Israeli intelligence. I'm surprised your father didn't have a go at Klemper himself.'

'He wanted to.' Judging by her tone, Maria wouldn't have objected to pulling out the odd finger or toenail herself. 'Unfortunately Klemper had become respectable by the time Father found him, safely under the Americans' wing. With that sort of protection the Israelis weren't likely to do anything about him. Father was going to resign until he learnt your department was looking for Klemper. Then he told me to establish contact and prod you in the right direction if necessary.'

'Presumably he used you because you've no official connection with the Israelis,' I commented, far more interested in the sudden realization that somebody at SR(2) headquarters must have been leaking information to Miteck.

'That's right. I wasn't to interfere unless you lost the scent.'

Maria paused and when she did continue it was with terrible intensity.

'You are going to kill Klemper, aren't you?' she asked.

'That rather depends.'

'On what?'

My answer had surprised her.

'On how well you treat me,' I answered, reaching past her to stub out my cigarette.

From the way she began Maria seemed disposed to treat me inordinately well, which made it all the more pity that this was the second John chose to start hammering on the cabin door.

'I don't like it,' John announced, not lowering the Zeiss binoculars.

'You and me both,' I agreed, emotion overcoming my normal regard for grammar.

For a start I'd never reached Formentera, the haven I'd been aiming for, something which had had nothing to do with faulty navigation by our captain. George Martin hadn't missed the lighthouses and sailed right over the island, he'd been instructed to change course by John while I'd protested feebly in the background. Maria, turncoat that she was, had sided with John, indeed had been more responsible than he. Once she'd realized her masquerade as Julie Aston was over, and I'd reluctantly allowed John into the cabin, she'd wasted no time in informing us of Klemper's hideaway at the Villa Rosa. A map spread in front of her, she had pinpointed the location in the south-west corner of Ibiza. For Klemper's purposes the situation was ideal, in one of the most underpopulated regions of the island on the cliffs opposite the islets of Vedra and Vedra-nell, the only access on the landward side by what appeared to be a cart track.

'What do you think?' John had asked when Maria's briefing had finished.

'It seems fairly straightforward,' I'd answered. 'We establish base camp on Formentera, hire a small fishing boat and use Vedra as an observation post until we're ready to move in.'

The baffled stares of John and Maria had been mute accusations of insanity. They weren't to know that since my brush with Ramirez I'd been acutely conscious of my mortality, had been running scared in the sense that I'd wanted to keep well away from Klemper until I was prepared to meet him on my own terms. Nevertheless, I hadn't been too scared to appreciate the logic of the counter-arguments. John had stressed the time element, that Klemper was going to move as soon as he realized Ramirez was missing, and that Martin could put us ashore under cover of darkness, a mere mile or two away from the villa. Maria had chosen to concentrate on the island of Vedra, informing me that it was nothing more than a great, bare hunk of rock rising a thousand feet out of the Mediterranean. I'd raised the odd objection myself but nothing too serious, which was why, an hour or two before dawn, we'd landed at Cala Vadella.

By the time John and I were agreeing that we didn't like what we could see, it was midmorning and the three of us, complete with luggage, were concealed near an old circular watchtower. The scenery we had no quarrel with. This was genuine Mediterranean, rocky, uncompromising and almost devoid of vegetation apart from the scrubby, insecure trees, the kind of inhospitable terrain which had made generations of islanders struggle for a living until they'd realized that the same geographical factors which had kept them in poverty for so long could earn them a fortune if it was neatly packaged for the tourists. Klemper's hideaway, the Villa Rosa, was the object of our combined displeasure, a holiday home converted into a bastion, as we could see from our vantage point half a mile away.

Apart from its size there was nothing exceptional about the villa itself, a sprawling, flat-roofed residence, two stories high and painted in pastel pink. The villa could almost have been the property of anyone; anyone, that is, with £50,000 to spare and a disposition like Greta Garbo's. For a start it stood on a small promontory, surrounded on three sides by high, unscalable cliffs which rose dramatically from the sea. If someone was fool enough to attempt the climb he'd find the outward-leaning strands of barbed wire at the top sufficient to change his mind and send him down again. Only a narrow neck of land, no more than seventy-five yards wide, connected the villa's grounds with the mainland, and this was heavily fortified as well. The ten-foot wall was quite an obstacle by itself, but the electrified wire which added another three feet to its height ruled it out completely, unless Klemper made enemies of a gang of champion pole-vaulters.

Although these precautions alone would have been more than adequate to guard Klemper from unwelcome callers, he was obviously a pessimist. The gates were monstrous, metal contraptions, opened electronically from the gatehouse inside, where a sentry was permanently on duty, revolver in the holster at his hip and what appeared to be a M–16 on his shoulder. This wasn't all, not by a long shot. In front of the wall a free-fire zone stretched for nearly a hundred yards — no trees, no rocks, no man-sized cover at all. To round off the defenses there were two outriders, armed with rifles which definitely were M–16s, who were covering the track leading to the villa and making occasional sweeps through the surrounding countryside. Even allowing for the five men inside the villa with Klemper, I was reasonably confident. Given half a dozen tanks and a couple of Phantoms for air support I could take the place in a week.

'We shall have to move in before dark,' John commented, lowering his binoculars.

'I suppose we shall,' I said sourly. 'Maria can send in the recommendation for my posthumous V.C.'

What John and I disliked most of all were the manifest preparations for departure which had been taking place in the villa for the best part of the morning. Shortly after nine a truck had arrived and since then Klemper had acted as foreman, superintending the loading. Among the things loaded had been three large filing cabinets, marking the truck for destruction at the first possible moment, the same way that the only other vehicle in evidence, a Mercedes, had to go, as it was almost certainly earmarked for Klemper's personal conveyance. Both vehicles would be leaving before nightfall, of this we were positive, and we would have to attack without the benefit of reinforcements. John, of course, hadn't arranged for any help, not knowing why he'd come to Ibiza until he'd rescued me from Ramirez. I had made arrangements — this was why I'd visited San Antonio Post Office the previous evening — but help would arrive too late. The six men I'd requested would be heading for San Francisco Javier, Formentera, where they'd be worse than useless, even after Martin had passed on my message.

'I don't like it.'

It was my turn to say this.

'Neither do I,' John answered, 'but we've established that already. We need to do some constructive thinking.

'Go ahead,' I said. 'Let's hear what you're capable of.'

'O.K. The way I see the situation we have four possible alternatives.'

'Four?' I queried, wondering whether he'd made a mistake in his math.

'That's what I said. First of all, we could simply follow Klemper when he leaves. Find out where he's going.'

John made this suggestion with considerable lack of conviction but the shake of my head was decisive.

'We're down to three choices,' I told him.

'I thought you might say that,' John grinned. 'Here's my second suggestion. We ambush the truck and Mercedes when they leave the villa.'

'If you happen to have a couple of Schmeissers and some hand grenades in your suitcase I'm game to try. Otherwise we haven't enough firepower to ambush a nun on a bicycle.'

'Fair enough.' John was becoming more cheerful every second. 'The same argument eliminates my third idea as well. That leaves us with just the one.'

'There's no need to spell it out,' I said. 'We have to go into the villa after Klemper.'

'Agreed.' John beamed.

Maria had been listening intently, no doubt impressed by our mastery of strategy and tactics. Now she decided to speak.

'How are you going to do it?' she asked. 'The villa looks impregnable.'

'A highly pertinent question,' John remarked, treating her to an indulgent glance. 'As I've done all the groundwork I'll leave Philis to answer it for you.'

They both turned to me, eager for me to spout words of wisdom. I lay on my back, squinting up into the sun, the pain in my ribs telling me I was in no condition to attempt anything energetic.

'How long before the truck is loaded?' I asked John.

'Fairly soon, I'd say,' he replied after a quick peek through the binoculars.

'Are they likely to squeeze all those packing cases aboard?'

This time John took longer before he answered, a thin edge of excitement in his voice when he did.

'They'll have to make two trips,' he informed me.

'Exactly. That's how we get into the villa.'

Ibiza, Spain, February 1972

The herd of goats completely blocked the road, making further progress impossible. The driver of the truck stuck his head out of the cab window, spat into the dust of the road and began to swear. The man beside him laughed, said something and climbed down from the cab. Still swearing, the driver joined his companion in the road and the two of them set about herding the goats into the rocks. Sutters watched them, amused by their antics and the language they were using, waiting until the road was clear before he advertised his presence. The two men were walking back to the truck, the last of the goats shooed away, when Sutters stepped out behind them, his gun pointing at their backs.

'Stay where you are,' he commanded in Spanish.

13

Our hiding place in the rocks was warm and concealed and Maria's presence beside me was a powerful temptation. Unfortunately there was other, more pressing business and I cautiously raised my head to see what the situation was. The two men Klemper had detailed for guard duty outside the villa weren't very good at their job. They appeared hard-bitten enough, squat, belligerent characters who would be proficient with fists, knives or guns in a street brawl but who were completely out of place in the countryside, moving over the ground with as much stealth as the Light Brigade at Balaclava. Now that the truck had passed they were sitting at the roadside having a quiet smoke, obviously not expecting to be attacked. Two very good reasons for their confidence were the plastic-stocked M–16 automatic rifles they had with them, weapons for which I had the greatest respect. Admittedly, they did have their drawbacks. They were too light to be much use in hand-to-hand combat, the lightweight stock tending to crumple or shatter, and the sights were awkward, so high that taking careful aim was difficult, the handler risking a bullet through his head while sighting. On the other hand, the M–16 had several merits which outweighed its disadvantages. Theoretically it was capable of firing short bursts of over 700 rounds a minute, although reloading meant the effective performance was a hell of a sight lower, more like 70 a minute in the hands of an expert. Then there were the unpleasant things the 5.56mm bullets could do to people who were stupid enough to stand in their path. Get hit in the shoulder and your arm was liable to drop off. Get hit in the torso at ranges of less than a hundred yards and the supersonic shock waves were likely to churn all your vital organs into offal paste. To combat this I had one revolver which was inaccurate at anything more than ten yards.

'What are you going to do?' Maria asked, sounding nervous.

'I suppose I could kill them,' I joked, busily calculating the route I'd have to take to creep up on them.

'Kill them?'

There was no mistaking the repugnance in Maria's voice. The way she was looking at me wasn't designed to boost my ego either.

'I thought you were the bloodthirsty one,' I said. 'You're the person who's been pressing to have Klemper killed.'

'That's different.'

I didn't challenge her logic or lack of it. This was a situation where guile was necessary and I'd never had any intention of killing the two men. Not unless I had to, that is.

'If you're willing to help it might be avoided,' I said after a minute, pretending the idea had just occurred to me.

'What do I have to do?' Maria inquired, eager to avert a massacre.

'Behave as though you've lost your dog. Wander down the middle of the road and shout for Fido to come back.'

'How will that help?'

Maria still hadn't appreciated the nuances of my plan, looking singularly blank.

'You'd be surprised,' I assured her. 'Especially when you've changed your clothes.'

Reaching inside my shirt I brought out the bikini I'd removed from her Air France bag. Once the two Spaniards had seen her in that they'd forget all about their rifles.

'Mimi,' Maria shouted, hands on hips. 'Come back here, you naughty dog.'

It was horrible, unconvincing acting, but acting ability wasn't what was needed. She was out of sight of the villa, not shouting loudly enough to attract attention there. The sentries had heard her though and, keeping under cover, they had moved to a spot where they could see her as well. This was where the Philis psychological prognosis should be confirmed. They were male, Spanish, men of violence and presumably scheduled to leave Ibiza later in the day. Maria was female, young, beautiful and dressed in a manner which made her one of the likeliest candidates for rape I'd ever seen.

'Mimi,' she called again. 'Come back here.'

Although she didn't sound any more convincing than she had before, there was a fantastic improvement in her performance when the two men materialized in the road, less than five yards away from her. For a moment she was rooted to the spot, mouth opened for another shout to the nonexistent dog, a look of perfectly genuine surprise on her face, then she turned to run, heading into the rocks at the side of the road, up to where I was waiting. It didn't take the two Spaniards long to decide to run after her, something which was hardly unexpected. Modesty wasn't one of Maria's noticeable virtues and the bikini did nothing to improve her case. The simple act of walking, viewed from the rear, made her buttocks appear positively prehensile. When she ran the effect must have been truly spectacular. I couldn't tell, having to make do with the front view, but the men chasing her seemed quite impressed. They were gaining fast, would certainly have caught Maria within another few steps even if she hadn't gone into the last part of her routine, pretending to trip.

Once they'd caught her the guards weren't quite sure what to do. Maria had rolled over on her back, one leg crooked in provocative coyness, her breath coming in great panting sobs which did interesting things to her breasts while the two men stood over her, looking rather sheepish.

'What do you want?' she panted.

The question was her own idea, such a stupid one I was tempted to leave her to learn the answer the hard way.

'There's no need to be frightened,' the taller of the two men told her, leaning his rifle against a rock and bending down to help Maria to her feet. 'We're not going to hurt you.'

Since he'd set an example my natural chivalry reasserted itself, inspiring me to intervene before he had an opportunity to break his word. I took the smaller guard first, the one still clutching his rifle, and tapped him carefully behind the ear with my lead-weighted cosh, plunging him into oblivion with the impression of Maria's bosom etched on his retinas. The second man reacted quite fast under the circumstances, relinquishing his hold on Maria's shoulder in favor of a quick grab for his rifle, meaning I had to hit him harder than I'd intended and without the precision I'd used on his companion. He was still breathing when I checked, but I wouldn't have taken bets on how long this state of affairs was likely to last. There just wasn't time to rush him to hospital.

John was sitting comfortably in the shade of a tree, an M–16 resting across his knees, as he supervised the unloading of the truck. His two prisoners were busy carrying the heavy packing cases to the edge of the cliff, whence they were dropped into the ocean below.

'What's the score?' I asked, hunkering down beside him.

'We're in luck,' John replied. 'The truck was heading for a warehouse in Ibiza, not a ship. There's no one waiting for it at the other end who's likely to tell Klemper it hasn't arrived.'

'That's a relief. I'd hate Klemper to know we're coming.'

John treated me to a friendly grin.

'Your trouble is that you worry too much,' he said. 'How did things go at your end? Did you take out the guards?'

'They won't interfere.'

'Fine. In that case we'll hit the villa in an hour. Until then we could spend our time going through those filing cabinets.'

He grinned again when I shook my head. Once opened the files could prove more dangerous than anything in the villa.

'They go into the sea, along with everything else,' I said. 'Klemper will tell us where to find Schnellinger.'

This was an out-and-out lie. I already knew who Schnellinger really was and had no intention of sharing the secret with John.

Bumping round in the back of the truck as it drove down to the Villa Rosa, I was glad I wasn't in John's position. I might be uncomfortable, but at least I was relatively safe whereas John was highly vulnerable. He was in the cab with our two prisoners, squatting out of sight on the floor and keeping his gun well in evidence. Unarmed as they were, the prisoners could still take him almost at will, once they realized how much bluff had been mixed with our threats. Before setting out, John and I had done our best to establish complete psychological dominance, explaining carefully, in great detail, what would happen if they weren't good boys. Not only would they have to worry about John loosing off his automatic in the cab but, at the first sign of trouble, I intended to use my M–16 from behind, firing through the thin, wooden partitions separating the cab from the rear section of the truck. At the time they'd been impressed enough, demoralized by our gory predictions about the consequences of disobedience. Once their brains were in working order again they might begin to wonder what fate held in store for them after they'd helped us to penetrate the villa's defenses.

With a squealing of brakes the truck pulled to a halt, showing we'd reached the gates of the villa, and I crouched by the tailboard, relaxed now that we were committed, feeling so lethargic I nearly yawned, a sure-fire indication that great spurts of adrenalin were being pumped through my system. As far as I could gather the prisoners had behaved perfectly, but from now on anything could happen and I had to be ready to move very fast indeed.

For an instant there was no reaction to the truck's arrival, then I heard the quiet whirr of the electric mechanism which opened the gates. A second later the truck lurched forward again in low gear, stopping once it was through the gates. Flat on my face, my right side pressed hard against the tailboard, I listened to the muffled clang as the gates closed and followed the sounds of the gateman's feet as he walked to the cab.

'You're back sooner than I expected,' he remarked.

'We didn't waste any time,' the driver answered curtly.

From where I lay the tremor of nervousness in his voice seemed painfully obvious, although the gateman didn't appear to notice.

'Hurry up and get loaded again,' he said, sounding as though he was turning away. 'The sooner we leave here the better.'

'Wait a minute, Nestor.' There was a touch of urgency in the driver's tone. 'Check the tailboard, will you? It's been rattling like the devil for the last few kilometers.'

Unsuspecting, the gateman sauntered to the rear of the truck to do as he'd been asked and the look of astonishment on his face when I materialized from behind the cover of the tailboard would have made one of the great photographs of the century. To surprise him some more I grabbed hold of his greasy, black hair and did my best to jam the barrel of my revolver up his left nostril.

'You look like an intelligent man, Nestor,' I lied, increasing the pressure of the gun. 'If you're very sensible and climb into the truck quietly, you might live to be a grandfather.'

Nestor received the message loud and clear and was very careful as he climbed aboard, helped by my grip on his hair. His repeated pleas for mercy, invoking the support of a galaxy of saints, offended my Protestant susceptibilities and, once he was safely over the tailboard, I bounced my gun off the back of his head, hitting him twice to insure he didn't wake up too soon. Leaving him sleeping peacefully, it took me a little over a minute to slip into the gatehouse, switch off the electrified fence and open the gates a fraction. Then, an escape route prepared in case of emergency, I reboarded the truck, prepared for the showdown with Klemper.

The villa was ominously quiet. I stood at the back of the truck, one of the borrowed automatic rifles held at the ready, wondering where everybody was. Klemper and two of his men remained to be accounted for and there should have been some clue to their whereabouts. Instead the villa was completely silent. John jumped down from the cab and walked over to join me, also to collect an M–16 for himself. The truck was parked behind the Mercedes, a position where nobody inside the villa could see us.

'The two in the cab?' I queried, my voice no more than a whisper.

'I shot them,' John answered unemotionally. 'Keep me covered for a second.'

Our precautions seemed superfluous. John immobilized the truck, tossing the rotor far out over the cliff, and still there was nothing to suggest the villa was occupied.

'It might be siesta time,' I suggested when John had rejoined me.

'It might be a trap,' he countered.

The thought didn't please me. While it was difficult to imagine how Klemper could have anticipated our plans, far stranger things had been happening to me recently.

'How about immobilizing the Mercedes as well?' I said, finding the unnatural quiet increasingly unsettling.

John shook his head.

'We may be the ones who need to use the car in a hurry,' he pointed out. 'The odds are still three against two.'

'Point taken,' I agreed.

It was easy to visualize a situation where we'd be glad of a fast retreat, even if I had no intention of going anywhere in the Mercedes. I had plans of my own.

'Let's take a look round.'

The first step was an outside reconnaissance of the villa, John and I going our own separate ways. Traveling on hands and knees was an especially undignified mode of locomotion for an adult, painful as well when most of the route was over rocky ground. Added to this was my justifiable apprehension that every corner and every window might conceal a potential assassin, something which made for a nerve-racking ten minutes before I met John on the far side of the villa.

'What did you find?' he asked, his lips an inch from my ear.

'Nothing,' I answered succinctly, taking the same precaution.

'Same here. Unless I happened to know there were at least three men inside I'd say there was nobody at home.'

We sat with our backs against the wall, both sets of ears strained to pick up the slightest alien sound. There was absolutely nothing to hear.

'It can't be a trap,' I said after a minute. 'If it was we'd have been long dead by now.'

John didn't deign to reply. I'd been stating the obvious and the remark was in no way helpful. Moreover, we weren't likely to learn what Klemper was doing while we cowered against a wall.

'There are only two entrances,' I said reluctantly. 'I'll go in through the verandah. You can keep an eye on the front door.'

Immediately John's face broke into a sunny smile.

'That's what I've been waiting to hear,' he whispered cheerfully. 'I knew, somewhere inside you, there had to be a hero waiting to break out.'

It did me good to realize his morale was so high. Although the villa appeared to be deserted I knew that it wasn't, that Klemper and a couple of his men had to be lurking somewhere inside.

Five minutes later I stepped into the living room of the Villa Rosa. It was an impressive room, running nearly the whole length of the building, and it hadn't been spoiled by overfurnishing. The white-pine floor was bare, apart from two calf hides which served as casual carpets, and the walls had been left whitewashed, the only decorations several wrought-iron Spanish wall plaques and three Mediterranean landscapes of no intrinsic artistic merit. The furniture, such as it was, was informal, a hodgepodge of unmatched chairs, obviously selected with a view to comfort, a curved sofa bought with a similar intention, and a venerable oak table which seemed strangely out of place. The only hint of sophistication was the bar at one end of the room. There were two sets of doors — the sliding glass doors leading to the verandah, the ones I'd come through, and another in the far right-hand corner of the room. This set was closed.

Silently, moving on tiptoe, I crossed the room toward it. Even now that I was inside the villa there were no sounds of habitation and I was becoming even more jumpy. After several deep breaths to calm me down, I cautiously pulled open the door and slid into the corridor. Directly opposite was a flight of stairs leading downward to the wine cellar and by its side another flight of uncarpeted, stone steps which led up to the first floor. Both of these I ignored, not interested in carrying my initial exploration beyond the ground floor and leaving myself with three more closed doors to open.

Thanks to Maria I had a reasonable idea of the layout of the villa and I chose the door to my right, knowing it led into the kitchen. This contained all the normal, run-of-the mill fittings I'd have expected to find in any kitchen, plus an electric dishwasher and an infrared cooker as bonuses, but nobody lying in wait with a gun, which was a distinct relief.

From the kitchen the corridor ran straight to the main entrance, widening into a small foyer shortly before it arrived, and the remaining two doors were on the opposite side of the passage to the living room. Both rooms proved to be empty. One was a study, containing a desk, empty bookshelves and clear marks on the floor where filing cabinets had once stood, while the other was a billiard room. Having drawn a satisfactory blank I opened the one door behind which I was certain someone would be waiting with a gun and signaled for John to join me.

'You can take upstairs,' I whispered.

John nodded, not particularly enthusiastic, and padded silently away, no doubt hoping he'd be as fortunate as I'd been. Once he was out of sight I nestled into a corner in the passage, midway between the doors to the living room and kitchen, a position where I could cover both flights of stairs and where nobody could gun me from behind.

When he rejoined me John shook his head to indicate he hadn't found anything. For a moment we stood looking at the stairs leading down to the cellar, the one place we hadn't checked, both of us reluctant to take the initiative. Then John broke the silence.

'It's your turn, Philis,' he breathed into my ear.

If I'd been walking on eggs I wouldn't have cracked a single shell, starting down the steps like a 175-pound hunk of thistledown. John had inherited my post in the passage, meaning he was only protecting my rear by implication, as, after a dozen steps, the cellar stairs turned back on themselves, taking me out of his sight. In any case, all the danger was likely to meet me head on, quite probably from behind the green door another dozen steps down. There was a keyhole and I had no hesitation in playing Peeping Tom, anxiously peering through to learn what was on the other side. The answer was a narrow passage which led to yet another green door. Unlike Frankie Vaughan, I wasn't inspired by the sight to break into song. Neither was I tempted to scuttle back to John and suggest we lay an ambush at the head of the stairs. Before I did this I had to make certain there really was someone to walk into our trap, otherwise we'd be behaving like a pair of prize idiots.

When I reached the second door I could hear no sounds of activity behind it, even with my ear pressed right against the wood, which either meant the cellar was soundproofed or there was no one there. This time there was no keyhole to help me and, undecided, I was still dithering when the problem was taken from my hands as somebody opened the door from the far side. For a long, heart-stopping moment we stared at one another in mutual shock, the other man, a pasty-faced lout with a crew cut, even more taken aback than I was. Then we responded together, with me squeezing the trigger of the M–16 just as he started to slam the door in my face. At a range of less than a yard the burst virtually cut him in half, splattering me with blood from head to foot and lifting him bodily from the ground.

Revulsion had to be deferred, postponed until later. Behind me the passage ran dead straight until it ended in a flight of twelve stairs, and there was only one direction to go, forward into the cellar. The body hadn't settled on the floor before I followed it through the doorway, crouched and ready to fire at the first sign of resistance. There was none, both Klemper and his companion, a young, good-looking Spaniard, rooted to the spot by the sudden attack, their frightened eyes switching uncertainly from the blood-soaked bundle on the floor to the menace of my gun, neither of them wanting to risk a similar fate.

Klemper in the flesh was a surprise, despite the fact I'd seen his photograph and watched him through binoculars; a drab little man, too small for the suit he was wearing, his gray hair receding fast at the temples, his weak eyes shielded by spectacles. Unless I'd known his reputation, I might have taken him for an innocuous clerk but, to prove he was nothing of the kind, Roger Brookes sat slackly in the cellar's only chair, head thrown back so that he stared sightlessly at the ceiling.

'You can come down,' I shouted to John, my eyes still on Brookes.

Apart from the plaster cast on one leg and a few slight burns, he was unmarked, but this was only to be expected. Klemper had been giving him the electric shock treatment in a last-minute effort to make him talk, and most of the damage would be internal.

'He's dead,' Klemper announced unemotionally. 'His heart gave out five minutes ago.'

Slowly I raised the rifle until it was aimed at Klemper's

chest, the only sounds those of John coming down the passage and wine dripping from the shattered bottles in the rack opposite the door. I had every intention of killing Klemper there and then, cold blood or not, only changing my mind when John hit me from behind.

Somebody was slapping my face. However hard I tried to dodge them the hands kept smacking against my cheeks, first against the right, then the left.

'Come on Philis,' John's voice urged. 'Snap out of it.'

With an effort I opened my eyes, taking a few seconds to focus on his face. When I tried to raise an arm to put an end to the slaps, I found I couldn't move, that I was tied to a chair.

'All right,' I mumbled thickly. 'Just leave me alone for a second.'

While I gathered together my scattered senses I took in my surroundings. The chair I was tied to was in the living room and, since I'd last been there, a new item of furniture had been added. The young Spaniard who'd been in the cellar with Klemper lay on his back on the floor, a trickle of blood running from a small hole in his forehead. He looked very dead indeed. Klemper himself sat in a chair opposite me, a half smile on his face although his hands were bound and there was a nasty bruise on his cheek.

'If I hadn't been so slow in killing Klemper none of this would have been necessary,' I muttered, my head feeling as though it was going to shoot off into orbit at any second.

'I suppose not,' John agreed somberly.

Considering the ease with which he'd taken me he was looking remarkably unhappy. Perhaps he didn't enjoy double-crossing his friends.

'Why don't you kill him now?' I suggested. 'No one need ever know.'

'I can't,' he answered. 'My orders are to take Klemper back with me. There's an awful lot of information he can give us.'

Mine had been a stupid question, the answer self-evident, but, however weak, the suggestion had to be made. Klemper wasn't worth one of us being killed.

'Why are you still here?' I asked, thinking of another stupid question.

'He's been trying to pluck up enough courage to kill you,' Klemper put in, a sneer in his voice. 'I offered to do —'

This was as far as Klemper got, the rest of the sentence cut off as John's fist smashed into his mouth for the first time. When he stepped away, turning to face me, John was breathing hard, but he managed the glimmer of a smile as he spoke.

'My orders didn't say anything about the condition Klemper was supposed to be in when I delivered him,' he said.

'What about me?' I asked.

'If necessary I was to kill you,' he admitted after a moment's hesitation. 'I've decided it isn't necessary.' He flashed another wintry smile. 'Surprising as it might seem, I don't think I could.'

'Aren't you overlooking one thing?' I persevered, hoping against hope that I could persuade him to change his mind. 'Once you step out of the villa with Klemper I have to try to get him back. One of us is likely to be hurt.'

'We'll just have to hope we stay out of each other's way.'

The conversation was finished as far as John was concerned. He was already hauling Klemper from his chair and I felt helpless as I watched the two of them walking toward the verandah. Tears were prickling at the back of my eyes.

'John,' I called as he reached the sliding doors, determined on one last effort at persuasion, then changing my mind as he turned. 'I'm sorry,' I finished lamely.

'So am I,' John answered, 'but it's all part of the job.'

A couple of minutes later, when I heard the Mercedes start up, I abandoned pretense, allowing the tears to run unchecked down my cheeks, the first time I'd cried for years. The tears weren't for me, not all of them anyway. They were for John. He had little over a mile to drive before he and Klemper were blown to smithereens, destroyed by the thermite bomb I'd attached to the side of the engine. As John had said, it was all part of the job, but this didn't mean I had to enjoy it.

London, England, February 1972

Despite the speeches, both Tate and Pawson enjoyed the luncheon, the reasons for their enjoyment very different. The function gave Henry Tate pleasure because it was in his honor, held to mark his retirement after thirty years' devoted service in British intelligence. Pawson, on the other hand, delighted in the irony of the situation, finding it appealed to his sense of humor, and he wished there had been someone with whom he could share his bubbling amusement. Eventually Tate had been able to extricate himself from the hordes of well-wishers and, with Pawson, had repaired to his club to continue the celebration. By eight o'clock, when Tate announced that he really did have to leave, both men were a little the worse for wear without being anywhere near drunk.

'You can't go yet,' Pawson protested, trying to attract the steward's attention.

'I'm afraid I must, Charles,' Tate answered, already on his feet.

'But I insist you stay,' Pawson persisted. 'We have some unfinished business to discuss.'

Tate hadn't had so much to drink he couldn't recognize the new firmness in Pawson's voice, almost amounting to an order. Still he refused to commit himself entirely, only perching on the arm of his chair.

'What is it?' he asked. 'As from today I thought my only business would be in the rose garden.'

'Not while Schnellinger is still at large.'

For a long moment they looked at one another, each guessing what the other was thinking, then Tate capitulated, sliding down into the chair. To give himself more time he fiddled with his pipe, filling it with slightly trembling fingers, but when he raised his head he was smiling.

'It's a fair cop, as they say,' he said ruefully. 'How long have you known?'

'Since Philis told me. However hard he works at hiding the fact, he does have a brain.'

The steward came to take Pawson's order and neither man spoke until the drinks were on the table between them.

'Philis is a hard man to kill,' Tate remarked once the steward was out of earshot.

'Cowardice plus a remarkably well-developed instinct for self-preservation,' Pawson told him, not really sure whether he was being honest. 'Philis trusts nobody because he can't trust himself. In any case, he says you were in two minds. He told me he thought you couldn't decide whether you wanted him to be killed or you wanted him to kill Klemper for you.'

'Possibly he's right,' Tate conceded after a moment's reflection. 'I never did like Klemper. Toward the end he was getting out of control.'

'Surely you're not going to disown responsibility,' Pawson interjected, a hint of disappointment in his voice. 'It's not worthy of you.'

'Oh no.' Tate sighed. 'I wouldn't do that.' He paused for a second. 'What happens now? Do I rate a show trial or is it more convenient for me to be quietly liquidated?'

'Neither, you'll be glad to hear.'

Pawson sipped his whisky, watching the other man over his glass. A few minutes before he'd seen Tate concede defeat. Now he saw him fight back, start using his brain again.

'You'd better explain.'

There was a new confidence in Tate's voice.

'It's quite simple,' Pawson said with a faint smile. 'A month ago a man called Beaumont was extolling the virtues of closer cooperation between the CIA and SR (two). At the time I disagreed, but since then I've changed my mind. The Americans have an awful lot of money and I'd hate to think of them having nothing to spend it on. They've grown accustomed to having a Schnellinger on their payroll. I can see no reason why I should spoil their accounts.'

'Go on. You have me absolutely spellbound.'

The smile on Tate's face matched Pawson's.

'As you wish, although I'm sure it's not really necessary to spell it out. I can provide you with plenty of information, carefully doctored information, needless to say. You can collect the money as Schnellinger, with a suitable handling fee. Then everybody will be happy, for a year or two at least. I like the idea of an American subsidy for the department.'

Tate was laughing so much his glasses were in danger of slipping from his nose and, despite himself, Pawson found the hilarity infectious. Briefly he wondered if Philis would have been quite so amused if he'd known of the arrangement.

6